T0117004

Absinthe

TO

Abstinence

Absinthe
TO
Abstinence

CAM MONTCLAIR

iUniverse, Inc.
Bloomington

Absinthe to Abstinence

Copyright © 2011 by Cam Montclair.

All rights reserved. No part of this book may be used or reproduced by any means, graphic, electronic, or mechanical, including photocopying, recording, taping or by any information storage retrieval system without the written permission of the publisher except in the case of brief quotations embodied in critical articles and reviews.

This is a work of fiction. All of the characters, names, incidents, organizations, and dialogue in this novel are either the products of the author's imagination or are used fictitiously.

iUniverse books may be ordered through booksellers or by contacting:

iUniverse
1663 Liberty Drive
Bloomington, IN 47403
www.iuniverse.com
1-800-Authors (1-800-288-4677)

Because of the dynamic nature of the Internet, any web addresses or links contained in this book may have changed since publication and may no longer be valid. The views expressed in this work are solely those of the author and do not necessarily reflect the views of the publisher, and the publisher hereby disclaims any responsibility for them.

Any people depicted in stock imagery provided by Thinkstock are models, and such images are being used for illustrative purposes only.
Certain stock imagery © Thinkstock.

ISBN: 978-1-4620-4383-5 (sc)
ISBN: 978-1-4620-4382-8 (hc)
ISBN: 978-1-4620-4381-1 (ebk)

Library of Congress Control Number: 2011913966

Printed in the United States of America

iUniverse rev. date: 08/17/2011

To my mother for her determination, will power, and faith
Love always

Every saint has a past, and every sinner has a future.

—Oscar Wilde

1

My shirt was soaked in sweat, my mind was a blur, and I almost lost my leg. Sounds like a war scene, but it was just an incident filled with stupidity, raging hormones, and a lack of coordination. Instead of talking to the cute German girls on the train that morning, I thought it was a better idea to bang on the window from the outside like a horny gorilla. Maybe my primal instincts would seduce those girls to come running toward me.

Banging on the window was like hurling my body toward an immovable object. Resorting to primal instincts proved to be an unsuccessful approach. During that act of idiocy, my leg slid between the train and the platform. Instead of fight or flight, I was still stuck in thump and hump. The seconds ticked down until the train was to leave, most likely dragging my right leg along with it. Becoming an amputee without earning a medal would be a disgrace, but maybe this accident would be somewhat humorous in the long run. I could rub my nub on people for a laugh, and I would definitely have made the best damn pirate every Halloween.

Before I knew it, someone lifted me out of the shameful hole of female rejection and onto the hard but safe train platform. It was some form of divine intervention. I looked around, but no one said a word. Whoever had lifted me out of harm's way was gone. Somebody upstairs was looking after me, but I wasn't in the state of mind to recognize it. I lay there for a minute, collected my thoughts, and tried to plan the next move. In spite of all my efforts, all I could think was, "Man, I am hammered."

This event took place somewhere in the middle of the saga that will unfold. There seemed to be a pattern of euphoria, unnecessary risk, and miraculous recovery. This book is not a glossed-over version of a summer trip. We were two college kids with a combined IQ of 54.

My name is Cameron Alexander Montclair. Like my initials spell, people call me Cam. I was born and raised in Ellington, Georgia, an old southern town where my family has resided for over two hundred years. I am six foot two, with a good build and red hair. I never believed in lifting weights, but I managed to stay fit by playing every sport that had a ball. I grew up with an inner sense of entitlement, something that would diminish later on in a continuous humbling process called maturation.

Why recount this trip for everyone to read? First, it is filled with some stories that I just couldn't make up. Their truths make them more memorable and funny than any kind of fabricated tale. Yes, there may be some embellishments based on selective memory, but I will hold on to my perspective. If I don't recount them now, they will fade as the days pass.

Second, I solidified a lifelong friendship. Jackson McKinley and I continue to speak of the trip like it happened yesterday. It is always a bright spot when we get together, no matter how long we've been apart. He helped me remember a lot of the trip, and he gave me his perspective as well. This is not just a one-sided version. Hopefully, the multiple viewpoints will coincide into something that is identifiable with everyone who reads this.

Finally, it may become reason enough for others to take a step away from conventional life. I can't think of the number of people who are afraid to reach outside of comfort. Is it really my place to judge another's sense of adventure? Not at all. But from personal experience, it is necessary to take a leap of faith at some time in your life. If you don't, you will regret it. Making excuses just means selling yourself short through fear and contemplation.

The idea of a major vacation formulated in the summer of 2005, when some friends and I were watching a soccer game on TV. During the game, all I could think was, "I could be watching the World Cup a year from now in Germany."

My mind raced as the game progressed. The beer would flow, I would find the Aryan race, and the cheering would never stop.

Jackson, my lifelong friend, was sitting beside me. Jackson was an interesting guy, to say the least. Boring was not in his short vocabulary, but loyal and sincere rang true.

We had many laughs as we grew up, even more when we started drinking and smoking pot. The word "party" was very familiar to both of us by the age of twelve. Jackson's older sister hosted many blowouts, and we were always welcome.

After the Friday night high school football games, many kids flooded in and out of Jackson's well-decorated and inviting home. During those parties, Jackson and I often grabbed a beer, and the liquor cabinet was readily available.

His home was rich with antiques and filled with Irish blood. There was an intriguing dichotomy of love and hate, but anyone in the family would give the shirt off their back to someone they cared about. Hell, they'd probably rip somebody else's shirt off of them as well.

High school parties were not a new discovery. The tradition had been around for generations, but this old southern town seemed to be just a little bit different. For the most part, my peers and I grew up privileged, and we took for granted the almost complete lack of responsibility associated with our adolescent lives.

Jackson and I went to different high schools, but we lived in the same neighborhood. Ellington had been a resort at the turn of the twentieth century. It was the farthest south you could go before the railroads started taking people farther down to Florida. Immaculate hotels hosted masquerade balls, golfing, fine dining, and fox hunts.

Even in such a classy environment, there was no doubt in my mind that these people were getting loose. It's hard to imagine the days when flaunting an ankle was sexy. It seems that a dress with a little bit of ankle showing was like having a butterfly tattoo on the lower back today. When a lovely whore of the early time came strolling through the room, showing those sexy ankles, all of the cigar-smoking and scotch-drinking gentlemen silently thought, "Bull's-eye."

Ellington had deteriorated over the years, mainly due to fires, racial politics, and apathy. There was still a sense of camaraderie, even if it was ostentatious. Families knew families, and privacy was hard to find among the gossiping stay-at-home moms. But my friends and I still found a way to have a mighty good time.

I went to a unique high school. It was the oldest chartered high school in the South. George Washington had visited, wig and all. It was three fourths black and one fourth white, including the poorest people in town, along with the richest. There was never a shortage of fun, and somehow the completely diverse class of students got along.

Fake IDs were rampant, and someone was always making a run to the gas station or liquor store. Buddy Applegate, another close friend, would go every Friday after school and buy the usual handle of Seagram's Seven and Sprite. By the time he was sixteen, the old Chinese lady behind the counter knew Buddy by name.

All of these facts of life in Ellington built upon themselves. Many of the early freedoms we enjoyed led us to believe we were more mature than we actually were.

———————————

After watching that soccer game and coming up with the idea to go to Europe, it was time for me and Jackson to start planning. Jackson was going to North Georgia College and State University, and I was going to the University of North Carolina.

That last summer in Ellington contained every typical way of saying farewell before going to college. There was a lake close by, and we spent hours tubing, playing drinking games, partaking in herbal treatments, eating fried chicken, drinking some more, and listening to Kenny Chesney. Kenny was always singing about summertime and beer, so it seemed right. This was Georgia, and a little cheesy country music never killed anyone.

In order to pay for the trip, I had saved some money from working at Home Cookin', a local soul food restaurant. It was an awesome job in high school and a rite of passage in many ways, although delivering comfort food to the nurses at the nearby hospital and getting tipped a quarter was frustrating. Common phrases included:

"Where my ketchup be at?"

"You done forgot my banana pudding."

"You bring butta for my cornbread?"

One time, a nurse asked me if I had change for a "hunned-dolla bill." We only carried seventeen dollars in change, and her total was somewhere around three dollars and fifty cents.

I always regretted not saying, "No ma'am, I don't have change for a Benjamin, but I'm sure if you swipe your credit card through the bubbling ass of your coworker, that would suffice."

In another implausible incident, Buddy took a house delivery, and a little black boy paid the tab with thirty dollars in rolled pennies.

Taking deliveries to the dark side of town was always fun. One day, I was making a delivery to a community center in the ghetto. When I pulled up to a stop sign, a crackhead lady hopped into the passenger seat of my car. She told me someone had just tried to stab her, and she would suck my dick for five dollars. Understandably, I refused.

Since I turned down a top dollar crackhead blowjob and this lady was obviously out of her gourd, I pushed her out of my car while sharing plenty of expletives. It was just another day working at Home Cookin'.

The job had many perks as well. Our boss, who everyone called the Godfather, was tough but fair. There were always people coming in that seemed to owe the Godfather a favor. There was never a shortage of deals going on outside. I remember one day seeing the Godfather measure out a bag of sugar for the sweet tea while humming Eric Clapton's infamous song, "Cocaine."

Please understand, the Godfather was not a drug dealer by any means, it was just a funny incident. Actually, he was a very standup individual in the community, and he seemed to run the café more out of pleasure than necessity. He taught us young boys to work hard and respect every customer regardless of their behavior.

In order to make the European escapade work, Jackson and I had to stay in touch and plan accordingly. To start our freshman year, I traveled north, and Jackson went into the mountains of Georgia.

Despite his raging immaturity, Jackson made the mature decision to go to boot camp instead of the usual party-filled college scene.

I, on the other hand, was fully immersed in such a social setting. At UNC, I knew one person. Girls lived on the same hall as the boys, and kids pretended to be adults.

The first night in the dorms, I came back at two in the morning to find my RA playing beer pong in someone's room. There were few rules, and it was a time of no supervision. This may seem like the run-of-the-mill freshman year, and in a lot of ways, it was just that.

There were fraternities and pledging, more alcohol and drugs, and there were plenty of girls who would have shown a shin instead of just an ankle back in the day.

There was football, bluegrass, and basketball. There were also sixteen thousand undergraduates and generations that had experienced the same thing. It was new and exciting at the time, and I wouldn't take it back.

I couldn't help but wonder if I was doing something different or was I just being like everybody else?

While I was pondering my purpose for being at school, Jackson didn't get any ass at the terrible military school. His head was shaved, he ran every morning, and he found some relief by escaping on his few free weekends to the University of Georgia.

As our freshman year continued, there was a simultaneous countdown to the beginning of the World Cup. We thought it would be a good idea to bring along another person, but nobody would commit to the trip, no matter how hard I tried to recruit.

I said upfront to the friends I had made at school, "It will be around three thousand dollars total, and you will have the time of your life."

Guess I wasn't a very good salesman, because nobody bit on the offer. Jackson and I were on our own.

2

The date of our departure arrived. I woke up in elation, anticipating the next three weeks as no less than remarkable. It was June 6, and the opening soccer match was being held in Munich on June 9. Packing consisted of stuffing everything I needed into a backpack. My mom and I picked up Jackson, and we all headed off to the shuttle destined for the Atlanta airport. Mom took a sentimental first picture, one that did not reflect the debauchery that was to come, but memorable nonetheless. I had my iPod, and Jackson had his dingaling to play with.

The strange thing about going to such a foreign place is the anticipation. At that point in my life, I just wanted to drink, drug, and hook up. The combination of those three can leave somebody wondering and speculating for hours.

We arrived at the airport around noon. Jackson's dad, also called the Doc, had given us some Ambien to help us rest during the long flight. He was the coolest doctor in Ellington, and not because he gave us sleeping pills.

Doc had a profound impact on our youth, and he was never short of a good dose of common sense, especially during those parties of the past. One time sticks out more than any other, right before our close-knit group of friends were about to go to college.

Understanding Doc is crucial to understanding the significance of the speech he gave to us. He was the most genuine guy you'd ever meet. He made house calls to everybody in town, and he was a caring and sincere individual. He came from humble roots, worked hard, put himself through school, and didn't know anybody that wasn't a friend.

But he had some quirks as well. Sometimes, his family would talk to him, and he would just sit and stare at the TV when it was turned off. Moments and moments would pass by, and there would be no response.

Every time my group of friends went for a checkup, his diagnosis was for us to stop smoking weed. Good advice (that everyone failed to heed).

At this particular party, there were about ten guys outside just shooting the shit with Doc. All of a sudden, the regular conversation turned into inspirational dialogue filled with belly-aching laughter and cheers. There was a little red wine on Doc's part, and each of my fellow partiers was stoned out of their minds. The gathering of the troops and the speech that followed went something like this:

"Now I've known you boys for a long time. You guys are a bunch of shitheads. But you are all good kids, and I got to tell you about this whole college thing you're about to get into. First of all, we got some soccer state champions among you. Ya'll were eleven years old, and you kicked the damn piss out of that soccer ball. You were still little shits. We got 'Big Leg' over there that could kick it a mile. Come up here, Big Leg. You could beat that ball up like damn Cassius Clay. All in all, you boys are good guys. But let me tell you about this whole college thing. You all are going to run into a bunch of damn liberal teachers up there."

Laughter ensued, and the Doc paused.

Then he regained his command by shouting, "Now, I'm not kidding you now, a bunch of damn liberals! They're going to spitting a bunch of bullshit at you, saying, 'You gotta save the environment, the government will take care of everything, sticking it in another guy's ass is okay.' Now, let me tell you something. When you get up there and start hearing all that shit, don't listen to it. You know what you need to do? Burn their damn houses down! That's right. Give them the bird, and burn the damn house down!"

Each person laughed the whole way through and cheered at the end. It was like Stonewall Jackson had been raised from the dead to rally the troops against the evils of a liberal education.

In retrospect, Doc was right in a lot of ways. College is a place of experimentation and discovery. "Which philosophy is right?" "Is there a God?" "Who am I?" Unfortunately, there are impressionable ears in every college classroom. Some professors take advantage of that and use it to impose their own personal views instead of encouraging a genuine thirst for knowledge. Other students sleep through all of their classes and avoid the imposed mental dilemma.

Ambien helps you sleep, and that's what Jackson and I thought we needed on a thirteen-hour plane ride. The usual boarding of the plane occurred. The flight attendants looked annoyed, and Chris Farley's debacle with the life jacket in Tommy Boy immediately came to mind. Drinks were served and we popped our pills. I looked at Jackson and said, "See you in the morning."

The funny thing about Ambien is you don't always fall asleep. I had a window seat, and the plane was cruising. There were a lot of clouds out there, and slowly they became more than just clouds. As I continued to fall deeper into this hallucinogenic stage, I "saw" a dragon flying next to the plane. That creature glided over the clouds, and I waved to him like he was an old friend. The passengers next to me, a thirty-year-old mother and her young son, saw the scenario a little differently.

After gazing at Puff the Magic Dragon for what seemed like an eternity, I leaned over to the little kid and said, "You ever puff that magic dragon?" The sentence was a bit misconstrued, but it sparked a conversation that was comical. Unfortunately, the small boy said he didn't know about Puff.

Ambien also distorts some emotions, and with my speech slurred, I quickly and angrily responded to the little kid, "What the hell, son? Everybody knows about Puff. My nigga Puff has been around since Peter, Paul, and Mary. Puff was running shit before you were born. Get your spoiled ass to the library and pick up a damn book for a change. Playstation is a whole bunch of bullshit."

Needless to say, the boy started crying and the mom went into some kind of tirade about how the innocent ears of her child had been corrupted by my vulgar response. I flipped her the bird and passed out with an inflatable pillow surrounding my neck. What a stellar example of maturity.

Next thing I knew, I woke up with drool all over my face. The plane was crossing the English Channel, and arrival time was just under two hours. Once again, the idealistic thoughts of what was to come raced through my head. The last two hours took forever, but the plane descended and finally landed in Munich.

Jackson's granddad had lived in Germany for part of his life. A personable guy, he made many friends, including Dr. Traugott (I learned in my German class that this name meant "trust in God").

Dr. Traugott sent his teenage son to Ellington as an exchange student. Jackson's family hosted him, and Dr. Traugott owed him somewhat of a favor. He owned an apartment in downtown Munich, and this became our home base for the World Cup adventure.

Dr. Traugott met us at the airport. As weary travelers, Jackson and I gathered our bags, and we loaded our luggage into his European hatchback.

The Autobahn is very close to the Munich airport. For those unfamiliar with the super highway, there is no speed limit. Dr. Traugott was an old man, but he knew how to put that puppy into fifth gear.

Jackson and I held on for dear life as we flew down that highway at over one hundred miles per hour. We were in a different world, and this was the perfect taste to get that adrenaline pumping.

As we entered the city, Dr. Traugott slowed the car only slightly. It felt like a roller coaster, and a funny combination of nausea, exhaustion, and excitement set in as the hatchback zipped down each street. Jackson and I had no idea where we were, and that lack of direction was a reoccurring theme for the trip.

Thankfully, the three of us arrived at the apartment alive. Jackson and I followed Dr. Traugott up the stairs and waited anxiously as he opened the door. My stomach did a couple of flips in retaliation for eating the horrible food served on the Delta flight. I had to take a major dump.

I politely excused myself and went to the nearby bathroom. I hurriedly undid my shorts and dropped an atomic bomb. Meanwhile, Jackson listened as Dr. Traugott explained the nooks and crannies of each room.

I, on the other hand, stayed in that toilet and unleashed the foulest bowel movement of my life. It was horrible and satisfying at the same time.

After wiping properly and flushing, I quickly found humor in the toilet that I so vehemently punished. This particular European toilet was not your old-fashioned water in a bowl, swivel around on a flush, and go down the pipe. For some reason, it had a platform in the middle, a tiny water-filled hole in the front, and the water came rushing from the back. It became known as the "Doo Doo Slide" and it resided in the room we called "Club Van der Dookie."

Jackson and I had a constant competition to see who could get a turd to hang onto the platform without going down; he won most of the battles.

After taking the dump of my life, I exited the bathroom with relief and pride. That quickly turned into embarrassment, as Dr. Traugott decided to show us how to turn on the hot water in the shower.

As Dr. Traugott entered the toxic bathroom, I looked at Jackson and said, "Dude, it is terrible in there." Jackson caught the stench, gagged a little bit, and burst into laughter. For some reason, Dr. Traugott never said a word. The three of us stood in the bathroom, surrounded by the rotting decay that came from my ass, and studied the mechanics of the shower's hot water. I was hysterical the whole time and turned red from holding back my laughter.

After Dr. Traugott showed us the large room with two beds and a desk, he left. I knew he smelled the bomb, and he held it against me for the rest of the trip. Jet-lagged as hell, Jackson and I had one thing on our mind: time to get some liquor from the store.

3

I had taken one German class during the spring semester. I thought it would prepare me for the trip. My naivety was rampant at the time.

On our quest for the alcoholic ingredient for socializing, Jackson grabbed the keys, we double-checked our wallets, and we started walking.

We decided to take a left to look for the closest place that sold alcohol. The road was fairly busy, but I eventually had to ask somebody where to go. Thinking I could impress them with my vague understanding of the German language, I said stopped one gentleman and asked, "Wo ist der lebensmittelhandel?" (Translation: Where is the grocery store?)

The gentleman looked at me, smiled briefly, and said, "It's right over there." (Translation: You dumb American, you should know Germans speak English, we almost won World War II.)

Further down the street, there was a grocery store on the right. As we entered, each of us grabbed a basket. Jackson and I did not think we were full-blown alcoholics, so we gathered some deli meats, bread, and cheese to solidify our beliefs. Down a couple of aisles, the alcohol sat waiting to be bought. First, we grabbed some assorted beers and decided on the liquor of choice.

Growing up in the South made whiskey seem like the only thing ever made. I had broadened my selection of spirits over the years, while Jackson stuck with bourbon. However, in this country, the price difference for each drink was amazing. Jack Daniels was ridiculously expensive. We took into account our budget and previous drinking experiences and decided to go in another direction.

After looking up and down the aisle, we found it: Jagermeister. It was candy in a bottle, and it was dirt cheap. We grabbed a couple of bottles along with some Absolut vodka and headed to the checkout.

It was still early evening, so when Jackson and I got back to the apartment, we took a snooze. I had set my portable alarm clock for a two-hour interval, and we easily fell asleep. It was one of those deep slumbers where waking up was next to impossible.

The alarm sounded, and we woke up, groggy, at about eight o'clock. Jackson and I took showers, and we put on our very American clothing of khakis and polo shirts. We enjoyed a couple of beers of Bavarian hops, and then it was time to crack open the first liquor bottle, which had been chilling in the freezer.

Everyone who is reading this should know about the process of pregaming. There are different variations of how to do it, but basically there is a lot of unnecessary effort put into getting pumped up and developing a buzz worthy of initial public social interaction. Some people play drinking games with cards, but we just did it the old-fashioned way and took pulls. No shot glasses around, no mixers, just liquor down the tube. We kept taking pulls, calming our nerves while also reducing inhibition. We were in party mode, and it seemed like the only sensible thing to do.

Since I was halfway around the world, I thought it would be smart to have a travel book to map out where we should go to have a good time. First place on the list for the nightlife in Munich was Kultfabrik. It had twenty bars, all in a segregated area, and there was bound to be vaginas flapping in the wind.

Kultfabrik was an old noodle factory that housed themed clubs, including Americanos, Boomerang, Cohibar, Matador, Metropolis, the Temple Bar, and Titty Twister. Each had its own entrance fee and theme, from R&B to Gothic, '80s classics, house, and Latin rhythms.

Our next task was to take the subway. The German transportation system operates like clockwork, but it was somewhat confusing. Despite our half-drunken stupor, Jackson and I read the foreign signs and made it to the exit for Kultfabrik.

Not caring particularly which bar to start at, we entered the first one in sight, a club with a Latin theme. Once inside, I went up to the bartender and asked for ten shots of tequila.

I looked at Jackson and sputtered, "Who says Germany can't have a Mexican flair? We used to go up to Chico's when we were younger, and this is a testament to home. Cheers, brother."

The bartender poured the shots with oranges and cinnamon. The combination was foreign to us, but Jackson said, "Fuck it," and I agreed.

One down, two down . . . five down. No throwing up on either part, but the alcohol rushed through our veins. There was no telling what we would have blown for a blood alcohol test back in the States.

It should be evident that this book isn't just about the World Cup. Throughout our time in Europe, there were many recollections of the past. Sharing what we discussed and remembered throughout the years only seems fair.

Hopefully, it will provide a guide to the attitudes we held on to so dearly. And I think a book with every boring detail about a three-week trip would be lame. So back to Jackson, blood alcohol content, and breathalyzers.

———

Jackson had an interesting experience with a breathalyzer in high school. It also depicts the backwardness of Ellington. A girl in the senior class hosted a graduation cookout in late spring. Her parents were there, along with plenty of beer. The cookout turned into a party, and the cops soon appeared.

Another one of our ditzy female friends tried to run and hop a fence in her overpriced high heels. One of the cops caught her and brought her back to the front door. At this point, the crowd split in half.

Ellington is composed of two counties, Garren and Dudley. Garren County is home to all of the old money. Dudley County was new money. Garren had crack cocaine. Dudley enforced a speed limit. All in all, there were two completely different responses when everyone discovered the police were on the scene.

The group of Dudley kids ran upstairs to hide in the closets, and the residents of Garren sat in the kitchen and continued to drink.

The cop came into the kitchen, and the hosting mom happily greeted him, saying, "Hey, officer, how are you?"

He responded, "Well, ma'am, I got a complaint from the neighbors, and I came over to see if everything was all right. This girl in high heels tried to hop the fence when I pulled up. My partner is dealing with her. She didn't look too smart."

Oblivious to the policeman's answer to her question, the hosting mom immediately popped another one.

She inquired, "Do you have a breathalyzer? I've always wanted to know how those things work." What an idiot, right?

In typical backward Garren County response, the officer said, "Sure do, just need two volunteers, one's been drinking and one that hadn't."

The tension rose a couple of notches in the room. As usual, Jackson wasn't paying attention. I actually wasn't drinking that night, so I volunteered to go first. I blew in the machine for a few seconds and it read .00.

Then the cop asked, "Who here has been drinking?"

Jackson immediately raised his hand and said, "I have."

All the people there thought he was toast. He walked up to the officer, took a deep breath, and blew. It read .21.

The officer chuckled, and said, "Boy, you're drunk as a skunk."

Everybody laughed, and the mom thanked him for coming. The cop that had been dealing with the fence-hopping girl was Buddy's cousin. They chatted casually and laughed about the events that had transpired. Another example of Ellington backwardness. That was the end of it.

Long story short, Jackson had little inhibition to begin with, but once alcohol became part of the picture, there was no holds barred. The two of us fed off each other's view on drinking, and we threw caution to the wind.

───────────────

After the earlier pulls of Jager and five shots of tequila each, Jackson and I embarked on the coveted search for the lower section of the opposite sex. I had developed this philosophy about girls after my first year of college. It was methodical and fairly successful. During the trip, I coached

Jackson on the ways of women. Little did I know, I was teaching a prodigy and slowly molding a woman-humping beast.

I was not shy in high school, but I never really dated anybody, and I didn't have a lot of hookups either. My skills were missing.

In the past, it was easy for me to fall into the friend zone, and I hated it. I was extremely insecure, but I never wanted anybody to know it. I created a protective sense of entitlement, and being a fairly intelligent guy, I didn't have much patience with people that weren't as smart as me.

Even though I held onto this belief deep down, I had enough personality to make people feel comfortable. But girls were still an issue. So instead of wallowing in self-pity, I tried to improve before I went off to college.

I bit my pride and read several books on how to pick up girls. Yes, it was pretty pathetic. The type of information I gathered was not the embellished version of the pickup artist on VH1. The star of that show proposed using homosexual magic. He also encouraged guys to carry a piece of lint in their pocket in order to get a girl's attention. He taught desperate losers to place the lint on the prospective girl's dress and then pick it off like it was some disgusting thing that she forgot to take care of before going out for the night. The basic concept was there, but a cheesy and rather creepy approach nonetheless. I found that it was more about general demeanor, teasing, and closing the deal. Alcohol was always a necessary social lubricant, along with a high dose of persistence.

Jackson and I had frequent conversations about girls. It was not like Jackson had never been with a girl, but most of his high school encounters were more luck than skill. I had no credibility in high school either, but I did fairly well in my first year of college. I developed a solid reputation, and I gained the macho respect of my peers. At least that's what I thought at the time. The fraternity thrived on stories about hooking up with girls. That's not uncommon with a large group of guys. The hormones are rampant, and some of the stories about hooking up were pretty funny. Of course these tales were embellished but entertaining nonetheless. We never considered how degrading it was to the girls on the other side of the coin. The more girls each "brother" went home with, the cooler he became. I fell into this mentality, and I counted each girl like a notch on my belt. I was young and impressionable, and it was a mistake to succumb to the peer pressure.

While we were at the first bar, I shouted instructions to Jackson: "First, you have to be cocky and funny. Approaching a girl is an acquired skill. You have to watch out for a girl's sixth sense. They can smell nervousness, neediness, and insecurity from a mile away. If you display any of these things, just pretend like you aren't, and it gets better each time."

"Then what do you do?" Jackson asked eagerly.

"Then, the fun starts. Find something particular about what they are wearing. Girls are very sensitive to appearance and always cautious about how they are perceived. Poking fun at an oversized bracelet, laughing at a short girl with high heels, or joking about the color of her purse are all good starters. But for God's sake, don't put lint on her and pick it off. If they don't bite, they're a bitch anyways."

"Okay, that sounds easy enough, what next?"

"Next, you can have a somewhat regular conversation, and then make sure to walk away. Tell her you have to get back to your friends, and you might see her later. It's right there in the movie Dazed and Confused. When the freshman kid likes that sophomore, the crazy older guy tells him to tell her, 'We are going to the moon tower with kegs. I got a ride already, and I might see you later. Sounds crazy but it works.' Creating a distance between your penis and the girl in pursuit makes all the difference in the world. It keeps them guessing."

That was all the information I could gather for now. We both socialized with everybody we could find, and the night flew by.

That first night was a blur for me. I vaguely remember dancing on top of the bar and Jackson falling off. He was an aggressive drunk, and he willingly flung his body in all directions to find some rhythm to the music playing. Unfortunately, he was highly intoxicated. The bar was about four feet high; Jackson fell off and landed right on some nearby stairs, severely bruising his tailbone. He couldn't walk straight for the next three days. I just laughed at him as he ached in pain. He rallied, of course, and ended up making out with a chick on the dance floor at the end of the night. Nothing outlandish, but a solid start.

Then, we had an incident on the way home. As we were leaving, we heard a group of people in front of us speaking in English. I quickly yelled, "Go America!" and ran up to them. Little did we know, these other Americans sucked tremendously.

One of the guys in the group was in the military, and the girls were just plain skanky. We made passes at the girls, but they didn't take very kindly to our attempts at conversation. They were as cold as a witch's titty in a brass bra.

In odd fashion, they started cussing and kicking both me and Jackson. Apparently, we were a little too much fun for the trailer trash trio. The resulting confrontation put a bad taste in our mouths for the American way. The guy from the military actually tried to fight us, and it was nothing short of absurd.

He got up in both our faces and started yelling, "I'm in the military, and I fought in Iraq. I lost a leg, man. I lost a leg! I'll beat both your asses."

The guy was wearing shorts and had two fully functioning legs as far as we could tell. Jackson and I looked at each other and started laughing. Either his post-traumatic stress syndrome was very real or he had a damn good prosthetic.

Jackson yelled back, "How are you walking if you lost a leg, you dickhead?"

The fight was about to start, but three German guys saw the squabble go down and rushed to the scene to play peacemakers. The Germans got in the middle of us hotheaded Americans before anything started, and Jackson and I laughed the incident off and went on our merry way.

This was a time to be cultured, not violent. Hunger set in at five in the morning, so we decided to go back and cook a drunken feast. The train ride back to the apartment was filled with repeated conversations and incongruous comments. The train came to a halt. After heading toward the escalator, Jackson and I exited to see the break of daylight. It was no big deal, and staying out until sunrise became a common occurrence on the trip.

Jackson was responsible for the key to the apartment, so he pulled it out of his pocket and unlocked the door to our safe haven. It was time for the master chefs to take over the kitchen. There was a pan, some olive oil, prosciutto, some random cheese, and a loaf of bread.

I heated up an unnecessary amount of oil, sliced the bread, and put the meat in the sizzling pan. Meanwhile, Jackson was hovering in the kitchen, acting like he was helping. It was similar to when guys hover over the grill and discuss when everything is cooked properly. Very manly.

After careful attention and concentrating on not passing out, the greasy mess was ready. It was delicious. Would I eat it if I were sober? Probably not. But at six in the morning after a night of partying, it was like prime rib. We had completed our first night in Munich, and we both happily passed out.

4

The trip to the World Cup had one extremely important characteristic: no agenda. We had planned a vague skeleton of a trip, with hostels booked in other cities, but overall, there were no plans. When I was a junior in high school, I went on a ten-day trip to Italy. It was planned by some teachers at my high school, and it was miserable.

Our group started in Naples and took a bus all the way down to Pompeii. Every morning, we boarded the bus at seven o'clock and rushed through everything. All of it screamed tourist.

When the bus stopped in Rome, we visited the Vatican. We stood in line for over two hours but stayed in the Sistine Chapel for just fifteen minutes. That one place in the whole trip was worth at least a full day of examination. The age-old brush strokes of Michelangelo were fascinating, but it seemed like going through an artistic fast food restaurant. After having such a rushed and unfulfilling experience in Italy, I knew the trip to Germany had to be different.

I adopted the approach of a completely carefree trip. In my mind, that constituted doing whatever we wanted. For me and Jackson, that included sleeping in until we were absolutely ready to get up.

Now, a hangover from hell doesn't make you a spring chicken either, but there was no real need to wake up early. Sleeping was just as interesting to me and Jackson as exploring the whole city in one day. We had three weeks, and that was plenty of time to have a full experience.

We woke up in a half daze from abusing our livers the night before, and it was time to eat again. We were surprised at how many Italian restaurants there were in Munich. Just down the street, there was a pizza place that we nicknamed "Guido's." It fit right into the budget.

This was a place where there actually was a language barrier, and we had a hard time communicating our order. I managed to order a pepperoni pizza. A greasy pizza wasn't the most appealing item at the time, but our stomachs were growling.

Then, I found a liter of Coca-Cola Classic. It cost three Euros, but I didn't care. I had grown up with Coke my whole life. The drink was memorable in every way, and that first sip always produced a crazy rush. I downed it quickly, and we inhaled the pizza. Coca-Cola was like a drug. It was especially tasty during the muggy and miserably hot summer days of the South.

———————————————

My first summer job was in construction. A family friend let me start working for him when I was fourteen. I was ambitious, and I wanted to start saving for my first car. This job was actually disaster cleanup, not new construction. That meant going into a house that had caught on fire, gotten mold, or had termites to prepare it for reconstruction. Every day at lunch, I got a Coke. It made the day worthwhile.

Needless to say, there is a big congregation of rednecks and meth heads in construction, and they didn't mind messing with a new fourteen-year-old kid. I was willing to help, so I just did whatever they told me to do.

On my first day, my fellow coworkers told me to get in the dumpster and push everything down. Like an idiot, I didn't hesitate and began jumping up and down on the old drywall, scrap metal, and wood. Not too long after that, a nail went straight into my foot. It hurt like hell, but I learned a lesson: Don't listen to meth heads.

The connecting point of these early memories is Coca-Cola. I always remembered it as a drink of a reward after hard work. It was something you earned, and it never let you down. I don't know why I had never tried it before, but drinking a Coke was actually the perfect cure for a nasty hangover.

———————————

That second day was the opening match of the whole tournament, and it was being held in Munich at six o'clock. Germany was playing Costa Rica. We had time to do a little exploring before the game started.

Instead of trying to scalp tickets for the game, we went to check out the Olympic Park, where the 1976 Olympics were held. During those Olympics, Israeli athletes were held hostage and killed. Jackson and I pushed that memory aside and relished the positives of the place. The park was appealing for several different reasons.

First, there was a BMW museum. All sorts of classic cars and motorcycles were inside. Jackson and I took some pictures and let the history soak in. We took a break from the party mentality, and the museum was pretty interesting.

Secondly, they had a fan zone. It had been set up like a theme park. There were huge projector screens set up for the game. The park had all of the amenities of a full athletic facility as well. Indoor soccer fields, swimming pools, and a full stadium were in the vicinity. There was also a putt putt. Jackson and I had time to play a round, so we paid the six Euros and tried our luck.

Incredibly, the three German guys who had broken up our fight the night before were playing there too. We waved at them and discussed the incident; they commented on our drunkenness and agreed that the military guy trying to fight was a douche. We shared laughs and wished them good luck on their round.

It was really refreshing to have a decent conversation with people from a foreign country. The average European has a little more on the ball than an American. For the most part, it is not hard to discuss varied topics. I think they are just used to talking about things, and they are generally not shy with strangers. This courteous attitude is evident in the South as well, but the conversations only go so far. These are strong generalizations, but they reaffirmed our preference for overseas encounters.

Jackson and I were not extremely competitive toward one another, and we just enjoyed the golfing activity. Once we were done, we explored the rest of the park. There was actually a good bit of trails, and many trees had been planted recently. One trail led up to a mount overlooking the city. We made our way up the trail to the top.

From the summit, you could see all of Munich to the north. Munich has the Alps to the south, and they were barely visible even on such a clear day. There were benches at the top, and it was an opportune time to take another sentimental picture.

I saw an old lady with a patterned coat on and asked her to take the picture. She snapped the shot of me and Jackson with big smiles. The old lady informed us that her name was Sunshine, and she walked up to this point every day from her nearby apartment. She told us that this park was originally flat land. The whole park had been made from the rubble left over from World War II. We were standing on grass and dirt that was covering buildings destroyed by bombs over half a century ago.

We sat on the bench, took in the sights, and paid some kind of homage to the many lives that were sacrificed. It would have been easy to say all Germans were Nazis, but this park showed a genuine effort by the German people to heal the damage from such a troubled time and revitalize a peaceful mentality that had been so severely distorted.

After having such a touching moment, we realized that the day had passed quickly, and the first match of the World Cup was starting soon. We had to be downtown for the festivities.

As soon as Jackson and I got onto the subway to go to the middle of the city, we could feel the energy. Everywhere we looked, we saw Germans wearing jerseys, face paint, flags, scarves, and crazy hats. We could feel the fans' pride for their country, and the expressions on their faces showed unity and support. Jackson and I were just along for the ride.

We got off the subway, and the streets were filled. Every shop and store was packed, and we managed to get a spot in front of a department store with several big TVs. The energy in the streets was contagious. I was so excited for this world event to begin, I had butterflies. I would have loved to be drinking right then, but I was glued to the TV inside the department store. I had goosebumps as both teams stood for their national anthems.

The whistle blew, and everyone watched in anticipation. A shot by the Germans in the third minute went right over the crossbar. A few minutes later, pandemonium broke out; the German striker, Miroslav Klose, nailed a shot from twenty-five yards out into the upper right corner of the net. It was the first goal of the tournament, and it was sensational.

The streets exploded into cheers. The deafening roar echoed off the aged stone streets and off the historic buildings.

The German fans jumped up and down, creating a wave of white, yellow, black, and red. I had a pure state of being that I didn't quite understand. It felt like time had slowed down into frames, but my heart was still beating fast. Overall, it was a high, and I wanted more.

5

Jackson and I were on a high the rest of the evening. Running on endorphins, we forgot to eat and went straight back to the apartment to continue our preparation for the night.

Jackson was ecstatic. "Man, that was nuts."

"Just wait until later," I responded. "We are going to the most exclusive club in Munich."

Munich was one of the most expensive cities in Europe. It was like a fancy and more historic version of New York. The beauty of the women was surprising as well.

The first day of the trip, it was like being on a Victoria's Secret runway. The girls were immaculate and abundant. Seeing the opposite sex through the eyes of an eighteen—and nineteen-year-old makes a difference too. Either way, Jackson and I would constantly one-up each other on who could spot the most gorgeous girl.

Every time we walked down the street, there was an overload of stylish women with tight asses, perky breasts, and perfect complexions. We didn't really have a way of picking up these random girls because we didn't have a point of contact. Instead, we just stared and imagined.

Many times, we saw these girls from the opposite direction, at a good distance. The unsuspecting girl would walk toward us on the sidewalk, and the radar would go off.

One of us would say, "Smoke show, straight ahead."

For about ten seconds, we would gaze powerfully at the oncoming girl. It was like a cheetah had spotted its prey through the high grass.

It became even more obvious when we turned to follow a gorgeous girl, with our heads swiveling around like the girl in The Exorcist.

I had not packed any sunglasses to hide my eager eyes, but it didn't take long to buy a pair. During these female spottings, I reminisced over the advantage of wearing sunglasses. They just let you look wherever you wanted for as long as you wanted. Forget protection from UV rays. That's just the cover-up.

I remember when we would have tailgates at school for football games, and the fratstars would all have their shades on. The dolled-up girls were hanging out in the front yard and listening to the band. The conversation was insignificant as long as one of the girls was wearing a low-cut shirt. She might go into a long story about how her week was going or which classes she was studying for last night. Do you think one of those guys was listening? Absolutely not. They were staring at the tatas like my Springer spaniel ogles a chicken breast fresh out of the oven.

Minimal efforts were made to continue the conversation by nodding and saying, "Yeah, totally agree."

Girls also need to realize that what they wear is their choice, and it is either going to create attention or not. I always think of Dave Chapelle's standup where he discusses the topic. Dave talks about a guy that gets caught staring at a provocatively dressed girl with some cleavage.

She snaps, "Do I look like a whore to you?"

Dave continues with a story about his response if he was dressed up like a police officer.

A bystander runs up to him crying, "Please help us, officer."

Dave pauses for a moment and says, "Do I look like a police officer to you?"

Classic.

———————————

P1 was the most exclusive club in Munich. It was a rooftop bar in the middle of the city. People drove Ferraris, Porches, and Mercedes up to the valet, and it was not uncommon to see celebrities. I had read reviews about it while planning the trip, and people raved about the great music and models. It was expensive, but this was the purpose of our slush fund. Problem number one, neither Jackson nor I understood European fashion.

We were elated as we went back to the apartment from the soccer match; we cleaned ourselves up and started drinking again. Instead of wearing designer jeans, leather shoes, and a sporty jacket, Jackson and I dressed how we were brought up. We didn't know anything other than khakis, polo shirts, and tennis shoes. Loafers were a possibility, but neither of us thought to pack them.

Like before, Jackson and I started out drinking some beer. The beer in Germany is heavier than the beer in the United States. It is tastier, and it makes Bud Light seem like water. After a sufficient buzz from the beers, we took some more pulls of liquor.

The buzz was strong once more, and Jackson and I began our quest for the elite nightlife. We managed to use the subway successfully again, and we got within two blocks of the entrance to P1.

"Cam, how the hell are we going to get in?" Jackson asked, muddled.

"We just got to have confidence, bud. Walk with some swagger, and it will be all right."

The entrance was inside a large cobblestone courtyard surrounded by four six-story buildings. There was a velvet rope and a large bouncer guarding a door in the corner. He was well built with a prominent chin and gelled blond hair.

Jackson and I stuck our chests out and tried to stroll past the bouncer, but he grabbed our arms, sternly saying, "Woher kommen sie?" (Where are you from?)

I tried my elementary German again: "Wir kommen von Amerika." (We come from America.)

The bouncer responded, "You are not on the list, and I can't let you in."

Jackson, drunker than the night before, exclaimed, "We're both kickers in the NFL, and we got rings."

"Not good enough; have a good night," the bouncer concluded.

Jackson and I turned around, tucked our tails between our legs, and tried to regroup. We exited the courtyard and stood against the wall.

"Fuck, man, what happened to swagger?" Jackson said with frustration.

"It's going to be all right, man, I'll figure something out," I replied calmly.

There were lots of people out on the street, and several different groups strolled into the courtyard while I tried to conjure up a plan. The guys in these groups had spiked hair, and the good-looking women wore tight dresses. After a couple of groups walked by, I had an idea.

"Let's just fix ourselves up a little bit, find some hot girls, and I'm sure we'll get in," I said excitedly. "We just need to find some hair gel."

Jackson started to get pissed and barked, "Dude, what the hell? Where are we going to find hair gel right now?"

"Follow me," I said as I started walking across the street.

As foreign as Munich was, it had been Americanized somewhat. While exploring the streets during the first soccer match, I took in the surroundings. I remembered that there was a McDonald's close by.

"All right, man, we are going straight to the bathroom when we get there," I ordered.

Bewildered by my determination, Jackson followed suit, and we went to the McDonald's bathroom. I pushed open the door and darted toward the hand soap dispenser. I pumped it forcefully and smothered my hair with the pink liquid.

"Are you fucking serious?" Jackson exclaimed. "That might be the gayest thing ever."

"All the Europeans are doing it," I rationalized. "We got to make a good impression. Come on, lather it up."

Jackson and I looked in the mirrors and styled our hair for the first time in our lives. Not sure what to do, we spiked it in some fashion and took turns sticking our heads under the hand dryer to finish the job. Our heads were caked in McDonald's hand soap, and we busted out laughing as we exited the doors. Now, it was time to find girls that would even bother with such ignorant Americans as ourselves.

As we continued back to the club, I stopped at a cigarette machine. I put my Euro coins in and a fresh pack popped out. P1. As Jackson shook his head in doubt, his hair didn't move.

Jackson and I returned to our spot just outside the entrance to the courtyard. Just as we arrived, a cab pulled up and four good-looking women, two brunettes and two blondes, hopped out. Without hesitation, I put a cigarette behind my ear and approached the otherwise intimidating group of females with my hair standing straight up. I looked like a damn fool.

I could hear that they spoke English, so I lowered my voice and said slowly, "Excuse me, girls, do you have a light?"

One of the blondes giggled and reached into her leather purse to grab some matches. She handed them to me, and I coolly lit my cigarette.

"What's the matter? You got a Gucci purse but you can't afford a lighter?" I said without missing a beat.

The blonde was shocked by my arrogance; her eyes lit up, and she punched me lightly in the arm.

I inhaled again, waited a second while holding eye contact with the sexy German, and said slowly, "Now you are already trying to grab me. I'm not just a piece of meat for you. I thought I'd let you come inside with us and buy me a drink first."

In the meantime, Jackson had walked over and started talking to the other girls. He claimed he was from Hollywood and had flown over to Munich for the soccer tournament. He bragged about our apartment and convinced them that his attire was the next big step in fashion.

The group of girls gave in to our ambition and intrigue, and we started to walk into P1 together. With a simple nod, the bouncer let all of us right in, and we ascended the stairs to the club entrance. Jackson and I thought these girls were a lock for the night.

At the top of the stairs, the ground was vibrating from the music inside. We entered the club at the same time but with different perspectives. The girls were obviously frequent visitors, but the trendy club amazed Jackson and me.

There was a large dance floor with tons of people moving to the piercing techno music while effervescent lasers shot in every direction through the dense fog.

There was also a second level, which was covered in sleek, white leather sofas. A large bar sat to the left of the dance floor with an entrance to the rooftop porch behind it.

By the time Jackson and I got near the bar, the four girls had disappeared.

We were so glad to finally be in the club, their disappearance was small potatoes. Like the reviews said, there were models everywhere. High heels and tight dresses exposed sexy legs in every direction. Jackson and I became intimidated and rushed to find more alcohol.

Standing side by side at the bar, I shouted to Jackson, "This is fucking awesome, isn't it?"

"Yeah! I don't know how we pulled that one off!" Jackson shouted back.

"Let's take some shots," I yelled. "Bartender, we want that liquor, baby!"

Thinking I was cooler than I was, I ordered four shots and two beers. The two of us said cheers, downed the shots, and decided to check out the rooftop porch.

The porch was crowded, but Jackson and I managed to find two seats. We had been on the go since getting off the airplane, and this was really our first time for reflection. It was a cool night in Munich, and we sipped our beers and relaxed.

"I can't believe we are in fucking Europe for the World Cup," Jackson said in disbelief. "This is a hundred times better than anything we ever did back in the States. Everybody at home is just going to be watching the games on TV. We are really here, man."

"I'm right there with you. I just don't understand why anybody would ever turn this down. How many times are we going to be able to do something like this? We waited a whole year, and it's here. I mean, college has been fun, but this is on another level. I don't even know what's going to happen when we go to Amsterdam tomorrow."

Jackson and I continued talking about our great decision to come and what was in store for the trip. Our minds raced, and topics of conversations shifted from sports to girls to memories of Ellington.

Alcohol brings out the heart-to-heart conversations. It lowers the fear of rejection, and people say things they would otherwise be too scared to say when sober. Many people around college age are just looking for someone to listen to them and give them advice. There is a very vague grasp of maturity, and idealistic rumination far outpowers a realistic point of view.

Most people that age haven't dealt with true hardships, so they feel invincible. There is also a lack of sympathy for others who don't meet the requirements for being cool. Just like others, I believed I was an adult, but I was still an adolescent. Deep down, people are confused, and carelessness is a way out of avoiding real life decisions. Jackson and I were in the heart of carelessness, and we would not comprehend or fully realize the moments we were having until later in life.

Our attitude of reckless abandon was tolerable at the time. We had no real responsibilities except to survive the trip and make it home. This freedom would create memories that were in an isolated and unique environment. Given our age and outlook on life, we would not be able to replicate our adventure at any other point in our life. The combination of timing and impulsivity created an unbelievable experience that has become unforgettable.

In retrospect, the trip was a true scenario of risk and reward. Jackson and I hedged our bets against a conventional and mature lifestyle constantly. It was like being in a big casino and waiting on the last card of black jack. No matter what we did, we kept beating the dealer and were able to survive. It was a thrill to tempt fate, but I was ambivalent as to when my luck would run out.

Becoming restless, I blurted out, "I don't know about this techno stuff, but I think dancing to it is the only way to get some ass."

"All right, let's get out there and show them some dirty South moves."

Jackson and I darted inside and jumped onto the dance floor. We moved, we swerved, we swayed, and we slid our feet back and forth. We found girls to dance with, and we were both sweating profusely. The McDonald's hair gel streamed down our faces.

I caught a glimpse of the DJ that sat overlooking the crowd. I pointed at the DJ, and he pointed back. Instead of staying with the girl I was dancing with, I climbed up to where the DJ was standing. It was too loud for a conversation, and nobody could see what the DJ was actually doing with his hands. Just for a laugh, I became DJ number two.

I moved my hands back and forth, pretending to change the songs and pointing at the crowd. They cheered. I pointed at girls, pointed back to myself, and continued my violent hand motions. I used the same hand motions Will Ferrell used in Night at the Roxbury. I continued to laugh at myself and completely enjoyed the night. I felt like I was the funniest guy alive. Nobody on the floor realized I had nothing to do with the changing music.

Meanwhile, Jackson was growing into his skin as a pickup artist. The girl he was dancing with was more of a cougar, over forty years old. She was a good-looking woman from Slovenia, and she didn't speak a word of English. After some touching and grabbing, they made their way over to one of the white couches and began kissing. They were close to the VIP section, and an angry Latino man stared at them, grabbed Jackson by the throat, and slammed him against the wall.

"¿Por qué está usted con mi mujer, cabron?" the man yelled. (Why are you with my woman, you bastard?)

Completely taken off guard, Jackson voice raised a notch and he blurted, "English, bro, English!"

"Rajaré la garganta esa!" (I'll slit your throat!)

In no time, another Latino came to calm the man down and figure out the problem. Apparently, the same woman had been in the Latinos' VIP section earlier in the night. The group of Latino men had bought bottles and bottles of expensive alcohol, and girls had been coming in and out.

The cougar played peacemaker, and she actually convinced them to leave Jackson alone. After that, Jackson was invited to share a drink with the Slovenian cougar and the lavish Latinos. Not wanting to cause any further commotion, Jackson agreed and sat down with them. He drank his drink slowly, and he and the cougar shared glances unseen by the surrounding men.

Meanwhile, I had no problems making new friends, especially after pretending to be the DJ. After I climbed down from the booth, a skinny, dark-haired guy ran up to me.

With a thick German accent, he asked, "Where did you learn those DJ skills? I come here a lot, and that is the best music I have heard in a long time."

"Practice, my man, practice," I said without breaking stride.

"Let me buy you a drink, my friend."

"Tell you what. I'll buy the next round."

We stayed at that bar until we were sloppily drunk. I stumbled back to the porch and noticed a tall, golden-haired girl sitting by herself. I was filled with liquid courage and sat down next to her, striking up a conversation. Her German accent was intriguing, and I felt like I could turn the conversation into a physical interaction. We discussed our homes and the excitement surrounding the World Cup. She said she had once lived in San Francisco, and I made fun of her preference for gay men. I can't quite remember the specifics, but I'm pretty sure I tried to solidify how masculine I was comparatively. This strategy was a blatant sign of insecurity.

In sloppy fashion, I had forgotten my proven approach for girls and continuously commented on her beauty. While talking, I repeatedly tried to lean over and give her a kiss. She shied away each time. Nevertheless, she continued to talk to me as I blurted out vaguely coherent sentences.

It was getting late, and most of the nightlife had died down. I convinced the German girl to leave with me, and we went to sit at a fountain outside the courtyard. In my drunken stupor, I tried to kiss her again. She refused again, and my persistence was causing her to lose interest. The conversation became stale, mostly because I slurred every word. I managed to get a kiss on the cheek before we went our separate ways. I returned to the apartment without Jackson and climbed the stairs to the apartment door. Luckily, Jackson had given me the key when he went after the Slovenian cougar. Finally inside after a long day and night, I didn't even make the effort to undress. I crawled into the bed and quickly fell asleep. Jackson and I were scheduled to leave for Amsterdam in three hours.

6

The alarm sounded at seven o'clock, and I rolled over in bed, letting out a deep yawn. I rubbed my face and tried to run my fingers through my hair. The attempt was halted by the McHandsoap from the night before. I was still drunk. Minutes later, Jackson popped through the door with excitement and energy.

More awake now, I fed off of the pep in his step. "Where did you go last night? I saw you with that hot older woman. You knock it out?"

"Man, we went back to her apartment and smoked some weed, and I nailed her," Jackson exclaimed. He acted like he had found the pot of gold at the end of the rainbow.

My inebriation facilitated my ridiculous response, and I yelled, "Righteous, bra! Righteous! I knew she'd take a bodacious ride on the bologna pony. I'm going to Club Van der Dookie, and then we got a train to catch."

Jackson and I grabbed our backpacks and headed to the subway again. At the exit, we walked a couple of blocks to the main train station. It was a Saturday morning, and the station was full of people who were not on a free-for-all vacation like we were. There were trains sitting in lines waiting to depart to cities all over Europe.

Before the trip began, we had both bought a EuroRail pass. It cost about six hundred dollars, but it allowed us to travel anywhere in Europe.

I had already gotten my pass approved, but lazy Jackson still needed to validate his. We went to the EuroRail section of the train station and stood in line.

My hangover was really setting in, and I nudged Jackson and said, "I'm going to get a Coke and something to eat. I'll see you on the train."

Jackson's nod was a good enough gesture to separate. After getting my food, I boarded the train; it was ten minutes before departure. I grabbed a window seat, and the attendant walked through to stamp my ticket. As the train began to move, I closed my eyes and slowly fell asleep.

———————————

I woke up and gazed out the window at the countryside. I looked at the empty seat next to me and began to panic. I had no earthly idea if Jackson had gotten on the train. Like being on a human scavenger hunt, I rushed from cabin to cabin, checking every seat. I double-checked but could not find Jackson anywhere. With five hours left in the trip, I ruminated over what could have happened to my good friend. He was gone, and I was pissed and worried at the same time. I went through a cycle of extreme anxiety and reassurance. My head was spinning, and I thought:

"Jackson got on the wrong train, and he is heading into Eastern Europe."

"No, he just missed this one, and he will be on the next one."

"What if he never shows up?"

"It will be fine; I will just meet him back in Munich."

I finally realized there was really nothing I could do in midtrip, so I calmed down and went back to my seat. After taking some deep breaths, I reached in my backpack and grabbed one of the books I had brought for the trip. Tucked away in my luggage was Jack Kerouac's On the Road.

In the book, two of the main character's friends meet in New York City and discuss their adventures around the country. The book describes the two as "the holy con-man with the shining mind [Dean], and the sorrowful poetic con-man with the dark mind [Carlo Marx]."

Without knowing it at the time, I had embraced the characteristics of both of these two men, minus Carlo's homosexuality. I felt a sense of urgency to do the unexpected. I had a good heart when I was younger, but

I felt like I had the right to manipulate others. I thought it just confirmed that I was smarter than them. It was not right of me to think this way, but it grew out of circumstance and self-protection.

In the back of my mind, I constantly referred to this trip as a liberating experience. I was tired of rules and restrictions. I was naïve but ambitious in my search for something more. I didn't know exactly what I was looking for, but this kept me motivated to look even harder.

Deep down, I was torn between avoidance and acceptance. Like most college students, I had been given the freedom to live on my own. I wasn't financially responsible, but this taste of independence only enticed me for more. As much as I convinced myself of my rightful ability to live without regard, I was running from my past and running from myself.

The Montclair side of my family were long established in Ellington. Along with prestige came many problems as well. Mental illness and addictions had plagued the family for years. Despite the problems, there was always an emphasis on keeping a good reputation and belittling any weaknesses. It was not acceptable to be vulnerable. The pressure to live up to these standards hit me directly and indirectly.

My dad had been killed by a drunk driver when I was four. My granddad on my mom's side stepped in to guide my youthful development. He was a very accomplished man, and I looked up to him in every way. He lost both of his parents at a young age and battled a physical ailment in his teenage years, but he overcame them to become a self made man. Despite his immense influence on others lives and his significant contributions to the community, he remained humble and sincere. He put many people on the right path for their lives, including me.

Even though my granddad was in my life, I didn't have a good concept of how to be a man, and alcohol and drugs were an easy outlet to cover up any emotions. I thought imperfection was unacceptable.

Inevitably, I grew up a lot faster than most. Death is damn near impossible to comprehend as a child, but I felt a sense of loss and equal responsibility to fill the void. My mother, Elizabeth, was a natural provider, and she exuded strength through her Christian faith. She made many sacrifices so that I would not feel isolated from my peers. Mom did everything in her power to raise me right. After my father died, she made a difficult decision to work for herself to make ends meet. It was the only way she could spend significant time with me as I grew up. I am ever indebted to her devotion and care.

With good reasons, Mom emphasized that drinking was like playing with fire. I was too arrogant to listen throughout my adolescence, but the words did resonate with an unaddressed fear. In my subconscious, my biggest fear was letting alcohol control my life. I was afraid of what it would do to me through others and personally. Nevertheless, my uninhibited behavior was part of my inability to accept this truth or the limitations that it included. On many occasions, I drove around Ellington while drunk, mainly out of rebellion. I projected an invincible persona, but I was really too afraid to face my biggest fear.

My body once again had repercussions from the night before, and I needed to rest. I spent most of the train ride in and out of sleep, and the seven-hour trip actually went by faster than expected. When the train pulled up to the main station in Amsterdam, I grabbed my backpack and climbed out of the cabin.

Although Munich was our home base, I had booked hostels in Amsterdam and Geneva. The original plan was to stay in Amsterdam for three nights and four days and then head back to Munich and ride over to Geneva for a three-day music festival.

As I exited the train station and emerged into daylight, my anxiety set in again. I immediately searched for nearest coffee shop, where I knew I could smoke a joint. Right across from the train station was a walking alley full of drugs and paraphernalia. I thought it was very strange. It seemed touristy, but coffee shops were supplying weed, bongs and pipes were for sale on the street, and people were selling drugs of any kind. This scene was the ultimate commercialization of getting fucked up. Everything was legal, and it was treated like a normal day.

I ducked into one of the coffee shops and went up to the counter to order. There were all the familiar names of very potent strands of weed. Like a menu at Wendy's, the sign on the wall had "Northern Lights," "AK47," and "Purple Haze" for sale. I picked out "Purple Haze" and some rolling papers. I sat down in a booth and eagerly rolled a joint. I lit that fat joint and sat inhaling it until it was done. I was extremely stoned, and the reggae music overhead relaxed me even more.

As I sat there by myself, I observed the other customers and began to giggle. To my left were two businessmen in suits. It was a break in their day, and they were high as a kite. It was foreign, and it seemed right. The weed was potent, and I had almost forgotten about becoming separated from Jackson.

I had booked three nights at a hostel called the Flying Pig. It was less than a block away, and I went to check in with bloodshot eyes and a goofy grin. The first floor of the hostel was quaint, with a smoking area to the left, full of chairs and pillows. A group of people were taking rips from a small bong as I entered. I received my key and made my way through the long room with a full size bar to the right. I slowly entered my room, which was on the second floor. There were four bunk beds and a bathroom. I picked out a bed, lay down, and fell asleep once again. I was just way too high. Jackson would surely show up soon.

After a quick nap, I returned downstairs to try to solve the problem of my missing friend. I went to the phone and pulled out an international calling card. Jackson had an emergency cell phone, but I didn't have the number; I needed to call one of our mothers in Ellington. After what seemed like forever, I dialed and got through to my home. I forgot that it was early morning in the States. A raspy voice answered the phone.

"Hello," my mom muttered.

"Hey Mom, do you remember the number for that cell phone Jackson has?"

"Why do you need it?" she said, more awake than before.

Not a very good liar, I responded truthfully but nonchalantly, "Well, Jackson didn't make it onto the train to Amsterdam, and he's probably still in Munich. Thought I'd give him a call so we can meet at the train station in the morning."

While somehow staying calm, my mom said, "You are going have to call Mrs. McKinley. She gave it to him before the trip. Call me back to make sure everything is all right."

"Yes, ma'am. Talk to you soon."

I went on to dial more numbers and connected with the McKinley household. I was looking for some answer to the problem, but calling mothers while they are still asleep to let them know a son is missing is not the best plan of action.

When I got through to Jackson's mother, I asked politely, "Mrs. McKinley, this is Cam. Do you have the number of the cell phone I can reach Jackson on? We got a little separated, and I wanted to give him a call."

"What's happened?" she responded. "Where is Jackson?"

It was easier to lie to someone else's mom, so I continued, "I decided to come to Amsterdam a day early to meet some college friends that are over here. He is coming on the train from Munich tonight, and I wanted to tell him where we will be."

"Okay . . . ," Mrs. McKinley said with suspicion. "Call me as soon as you talk to him. Here is the number."

I had the cell phone number in hand, and now there was no doubt I would speak to Jackson soon. I tried to dial the number several times, but the damn thing didn't work. Also, I was too stoned to realize that my conflicting stories about Jackson's whereabouts would eventually create frenzy in Ellington. I had reached a crossroad. I concluded that this was one of the highlights of the trip, and I was not going to let the situation ruin it.

———————————

Earlier in the Flying Pig, I met two girls from the University of Kentucky and four guys from Vanderbilt. They were going out on the town, and I was damned if I was going to sit around the first night in Amsterdam and worry. These college kids were sitting at the bar in the hostel, and I went over to them to start drinking for the night. We watched one of the anticipated soccer games between Argentina and the Ivory Coast.

The four guys from Vanderbilt were not as cool as they thought they were. I was tolerant, and I figured spending one night of socializing couldn't hurt. Besides, they talked of going to a nearby absinthe bar. The girls from Kentucky weren't half bad looking either. When the game was over, we grew weary of the hostel's bar and walked out of the Flying Pig and into the vibrant streets of Amsterdam.

"Man, have you been to the Red Light District?" one of the preppy Vanderbilt guys asked.

"No, I haven't gotten over there yet. I just got here today, and fucking prostitutes was not my top priority," I responded crassly.

"Dude, you got to check it out! I banged a smoking hot babe last night," the same guy said, like it was an accomplishment. This statement reaffirmed his lackluster personality and insights on life. Paying for sex did not impress me.

"So how about this absinthe bar? I can dig that." I remarked with a half smile. I walked with the group but was not in the same frame of mind. I believed in making friends from all walks of life, but I was quick to judge and put a mental wall up to those I didn't like.

The seven of us turned the corner and approached a white building with stairs leading down to the basement. I was unsure how they had found such a place, but I was eager to go inside. We descended the stairs and opened the old wooden door.

The room was small, and it had a bar on the left with two people working. The group ordered shots, and I stayed at the bar while the others went to a corner table to sit. Next to me was a guy with a scruffy beard wearing jeans and a plaid shirt. He had been sitting there when we walked in, and he was probably five years older than me.

"I want to try this absinthe," I addressed the young fellow. "Is it worth it?"

"Absolutely," he answered. "Here, let me buy you one."

Not one to turn down a drink, I agreed, and the man asked the bartender for the mysterious drink. She found two glasses and put them on the bar. She then poured a bright green liquid, put a sugar cube on a metal grated spoon above the glass, and lit it on fire. My new drinking buddy dumped his flaming sugar cube into his drink, and I repeated the motion.

"Cheers, my friend," the man said in a genuine voice.

We gulped down the drink, and the bartender brought over two Heinekens.

"Thanks for the drinks," I said. "My name is Cam."

"Martin," the man responded as we shook hands. "Nice to meet you. So what brings you here?"

"Well, I came with that group over there, but they aren't the most enlightened people. The guys are dicks and the girls are sluts."

By this time, both of the girls from Kentucky were already making out with two of the Vanderbilt guys. Martin picked up on this quickly and offered me some advice.

"American girls are the easiest. Think about a scale of one to ten. American girls are a one. Pretty slutty, right?"

I agreed, and he continued, "Now European girls and Asian girls are a whole different story. European girls are like a six. It takes some work to get ahold of them."

I was all ears. I took another sip of my Heineken and asked, "What do you mean?"

Martin continued, "They are harder to catch. Most European woman will not sleep with you right away. You have to court them, and they are much more demanding. Very rewarding though."

"And Asians?" I continued asking.

"Oh man. The Asians are a like a nine. They are the hardest to get laid. It takes a lot of work with them. The pursuit may seem like forever, but they are the most loyal of all."

"That's some good advice," I said, surprised. "I never really thought of it that way. There are some beautiful women in Europe, but now I understand where you're coming from. That makes me feel better about a German broad in Munich."

I bought the next round of absinthe, and we continued to talk about girls, politics, and culture. I was beginning to feel the hallucinogenic affect of the absinthe, and it coincided with the waning marijuana high from earlier in the day. We even got a good laugh out of the missing Jackson. I was too altered to worry about Jackson, so I found humor in it instead. Martin was much more fascinating than the people I had come with.

The Kentucky sluts and Vanderbilt dicks left the bar before I was ready to go. I knew my way back to the hostel so I let them go.

In a drunken but alert state, I said good-bye to Martin and made my way through the streets of Amsterdam. The multicolored buildings reminded me of Charleston, and the interconnected canals brought back memories of Venice. There were people riding on bikes over the many bridges, and I observed them as I walked beside the glistening water.

At that moment, there wasn't much introspection into the whys and hows of life. I was relatively calm, and the hallucinogenic effects were minor but enough to be enjoyable. During my late night walk, I did relish some memories of college fun.

Absinthe was different. Its effect was recognizable, but nowhere as intense as my first experience with mushrooms. During the spring semester at college, I was beginning to experiment more. I had never tried mushrooms before, and I felt that early spring was the time to do it. I had developed two close friends through the fraternity, nicknamed Gator and Bueller. The two fit right into my criteria for a good friend.

Gator came from a small conservative town in eastern North Carolina. He was well mannered, raised by a caring family, but boy, did he have a wild side. Gator wasn't afraid to say what was on his mind at any time. The things that came out of his mouth were irrational, filled with country wit, and profound all at the same time. He was a burly guy, and he wasn't afraid of intimidating other people to get his way. This was something I appreciated, and it was a challenge for me to keep up with Gator's lifestyle.

Bueller was the counterbalance to Gator in my life. He came from a small town in southern North Carolina, and he had a more progressive view of life. He came from a loving family as well, and his parents used to be hippies. They were much more open to liberal ideas, and this was appealing to me as well.

Bueller went to a prestigious boarding school in Virginia and excelled at athletics, just as I had done in Ellington. Bueller was friendly to everyone and had a strong sense of justice, especially for the underdog. His good looks and smooth demeanor made him approachable to anyone, and he was never short on girls. This was another challenge that I tried to match.

Drugs were readily available in Chapel Hill. It was not uncommon for students to strike up a conversation with a classmate that led to the topic of drugs and where to find them. It was rampant in the fraternity as well. A tremendous amount of disposable income meant that everything under the sun came through the houses.

Gator had run across some mushrooms. He was experienced in that area, and I was eager to get in on the deal. Word spread to Bueller, and since he had never tried them either, he wanted in as well. We all agreed to get away for the night to take the mushrooms. Bueller's parents were skiing, and he offered his house as a place to have the experience. The three of us got into my navy Honda Accord early Friday evening and headed south for the hour-long trip, smoking bowls of pot the whole way.

Bueller's house was the perfect spot to do mushrooms. I was hesitant about trying them, and I wanted to be in a controlled environment. The house had a sizeable front porch with wicker furniture and manicured vines, a vegetable garden, and a chicken pen for eggs. It was organic in every sense of the word.

Instead of eating the mushrooms right away, we steeped them into a tea. As we brewed it carefully, we talked with each other in excitement and anticipation. When the mushroom tea was ready, we each poured a cup and sat on the front porch. Bueller picked out a bluegrass CD by Jerry Garcia and David Grisman, and he played it just loud enough to be heard. As we sipped the tea, the effects slowly set in. Then things started getting weird.

"You see that shadow moving? What is that shit?" Bueller said, wide-eyed.

"Calm down, dude. Just let it sink in," Gator remarked wisely.

"Am I crying? My eyes are watering, but I can't tell if I'm crying. I don't know, man, I got to get out of here. I got to get out of here," Bueller said in panic.

Bueller got up from the porch and paced back and forth through the front yard. He started talking to himself in different voices, and Gator and I watched in awe.

"He is really wigging out," I said. "What should we do?"

By this time, Gator had hopped off the porch, busted through the bushes, and ran to sit underneath a small magnolia tree. Not wanting to freak out from Bueller's bizarre reaction, I followed Gator and sat next to him under the tree.

"This is really trippy, man," I said slowly. "I feel like the trees have morphed, and we are in some other world. It's like we have a better insight to how the earth works. It's all part of nature, and we are just in it."

I was way out there.

Gator agreed, and we went on to talk very philosophically as the music echoed from the porch. The bluegrass version of "Friend of the Devil" struck an eerie but enticing chord in my thought process. We were totally immersed in the hallucinogenic experience, and each of us fully embraced the other worldly perspective.

After talking for an unknown period of time, Gator and I went into the house to look for Bueller. When we opened the front door, we saw him sprawled out, face down, on the floor. I went over to wake him up, and as my hand got near his shoulder, he sprang to life.

"Dude, what the hell just happened?" Bueller said in confusion.

"I don't know man, but you are trippin' your balls off. You were doing some strange shit back there," I said as we tried to regroup.

"We got to go explore," Gator interjected. "Let's go check out those mothafuckin chickens."

With our curiosity stronger than our reluctance, Bueller and I agreed, and we crept around the side of the house to get close to the chicken pen. As we got closer, a rooster crowed, making the trip even more intense.

Through the back corner of the yard, we could see a church. It had a big white cross on top. I stood in front of the church for what seemed like an eternity. Just a minute ago, I could hear the lyrics, "the friend of the devil is a friend of mine," and now I was in front of a freaking church. I didn't know what was good or bad. I couldn't grasp right and wrong. I stood there paralyzed, not knowing which direction to go next. My friends seemed to have disappeared until I heard their voices from far off.

"Cam! What in God's name are you doing?" Gator yelled.

"Yeah, man. Get the hell over here," Bueller added.

I just heard "God" and "hell" within twenty seconds while staring at the huge cross on mushrooms. My mind was about to explode so I just ran into the safety of my friends and the house.

Once we were inside, I tried to regain my composure. It had been several hours since we drank the tea, and I needed to use the bathroom. I went into the bathroom to urinate. There was a mirror above the sink, and I was absolutely terrified to look into it. After some deep breaths and splashing some water on my face, I returned to my friends again.

As the night went on, Gator sat in the living room and suggested smoking a bowl. The conversations had grown from absurd to cordial and sophisticated. We lit the bowl and passed it around accordingly. I asked Gator some personal questions.

"Why do you do these mushrooms, man?" I asked him. "This just gives me a whole new outlook on life. I mean, what's it like to go to a concert while being on this stuff?"

The question hit an emotional chink in Gator's armor, an aspect that he rarely revealed.

He said softly, "It's the only time I feel at peace."

As rough as Gator seemed to other people, I realized that he was intelligent and troubled by things in the world. Gator struggled to understand and accept people because he saw right through them, a key attribute to success but equally dissatisfying.

Keeping his guard up, Gator made some more small talk and decided that everyone should go to sleep. We were exhausted from the mind-blowing experience and went upstairs to climb into bed as the sun was rising.

7

The next morning, while I was sitting in the smoking lounge of the hostel, I tried to create a plan of action to find Jackson. As I took a bong rip, I had an idea. I figured that I could somehow calculate where Jackson was by looking at the routing numbers for the trains. I'm sure smoking weed didn't have anything to do with that brilliant rationale. As I got ready to leave for the train station, Jackson walked right through the front door of the hostel.

I just stared at him and said, "You motherfucker."

The two of us couldn't help but laugh. Jackson had already bought hash, weed, and some white pills from a sketchy black man. We walked over to the smoking area and ripped a bong. Stoned but aggressive, I started to grill Jackson on what had happened.

"Man, you're a fucking idiot. Why didn't you get on the train?" I asked, somewhat argumentatively.

"I got confused with that EuroRail shit. I was exhausted, so I just went back to the apartment and slept. Then, I just caught an overnight train up here."

I thought about it for a second and remarked, "Well, you are a fucking jackass. I'm tired, so I'm going back to bed. Wake me up in an hour."

The hour passed by quickly. Jackson decided to stay in the smoking lounge and smoke himself retarded. While I slept, he entered the room quietly and nudged me to wake me up.

In a quiet, stoned voice, he said, "Hey man, time to get up and check out the city."

I stretched and rolled out of bed. We made our way back down the stairs and took one more hit before leaving the Flying Pig for the day. Smoking reefer was something we enjoyed from a young age, and we wanted to fully utilize the opportunity even though it reduced our resulting production levels and cognition.

The streets were bustling. Amsterdam is a very active city, and there are different forms of transportation everywhere. Bicycles sped by, trams ran throughout the squares, and cars came from every direction. The main square was about a block away. Our mission for the day was to make it to the Van Gogh Museum, but we were delayed by a quite unusual encounter.

As we entered the main square, we saw a slightly rotund fellow about our age galloping toward us; he looked really familiar. Jackson and I caught a glimpse of him about fifty yards away as he bounced up and down.

"Is that Billy Football?" I asked in disbelief.

"Holy shit! There is no way that is him. How the hell would we run into someone from Ellington in Amsterdam?" Jackson said in equal disarray.

Sure enough, it was Billy Football, not quite the smartest guy you would ever meet.

Well, good ol' Billy Football went to the Catholic high school in town. He was not a stellar athlete by any means, but his enthusiasm was always at the absolute maximum. He would beat his helmet in excitement after a three-yard quarterback draw. We had absolutely no idea what he was doing in Amsterdam.

Jackson and I approached Billy Football in slow motion.

He blurted out, "Hey fellas, how's it going?" He swayed back and forth with a tremendous amount of nervous energy, the exact opposite of how Jackson and I felt at the time.

"Uh, nothing man," Jackson managed to get out. "Just hanging out in Amsterdam."

Stating the obvious seemed like a legitimate answer. I just stared at him; I could not really believe what was occurring.

"Well, I have been working over in London, and I flew in for a couple of days," Billy continued.

He could not stop swaying back and forth with his hands on his hips. I was still staring.

Trying to wrap it up somehow, Jackson continued, "Well, all right, man, we got some sight seeing to do. Guess we'll see you later."

"All right, guys. See ya."

Billy Football shuffled past us and off into the crowd of people.

Jackson and I walked away, and I was in a haze for a good five minutes.

I finally gathered my thoughts and had to ask Jackson for confirmation, "Did that really just happen?"

I was thoroughly confused.

"Yeah, man, I think it did," Jackson responded. "What are the fucking chances of that?"

"I don't know, dude, but that was wigging me out. That was way more enthusiasm than I was ready for."

We were halfway across the world, and we run into the most random person possible. I had heard from other people in Ellington that when they travel, they always run into people they know. I didn't believe that, but this incident proved it true. Being under the influence of the most potent ganja in the world made the encounter even more ridiculous. Talk about a buzz kill. It's not like I wasn't still high, it was just one of those things that you read way too far into. After a vivid discussion of the absurdity that had occurred, Jackson and I made our way to the museum.

We were typical tourists, and we had the map out in full force. It was mentally challenging to figure out basic directions, but we managed; I became quite absent-minded when I smoked.

At one point, I stood still to examine the map. Little did I know, I was standing on the trolley tracks, and a trolley was about to run my ass over. Jackson turned at the last second, yelled, and I jumped out of the way. This was not to be my only encounter with serious injury. Maybe this strategy of getting as high as possible was not the best idea. I didn't even take it into consideration, and I just laughed it off.

The Van Gogh Museum stood in front of us, and we got in line to enter the modern building. There were a lot of lines there. We paid the entrance fee and began to examine the artwork. There was an interesting quote written on the wall of the first room. It read:

It is better to be high-spirited even though one makes more mistakes, than to be narrow-minded and all too prudent."—Vincent Van Gogh

It was so crowded in the museum, people moved in a single line around each wall to look at the masterpieces. There were other people our age, and they were definitely under the influence of something as well.

Jackson and I were in the zone, and we fully adopted a snobbish attitude while critically examining the art. We tried to interpret several paintings, and we looked at some on our own. Putting our hands up and stroking our chins seemed appropriate. I looked at a painting, and the painting looked back at me. We spent a good hour and a half there, and we soon lost our focus, wanting to move on. Our high was wearing off as well.

It was a gorgeous day, and there was a large park in the middle of the city. What better way to enjoy ourselves than just taking a stroll. We made our way to the edge of the park, and there was another coffee shop on the corner. We got distracted once again. But when you have no agenda, it really doesn't hamper the trip in any way. We switched our plans on the fly, and it was so much easier than following a schedule.

As we approached the coffee shop, there was a sweet old lady in a wheelchair. That grandma was wrinkly as a prune, but she had a wide smile on her face. She had to be ninety years old, and she sat there soaking in the sun. She probably realized death was around the corner and wanted to enjoy her waning days.

Then, a younger lady walked out of the coffee shop and handed the grandma a huge joint. Without hesitation, the little old lady lit that bad boy up. The Ganja Grandma sat in her wheelchair and got high as hell. Once again, ridiculous.

This was our fourth day in Europe, and as each day passed, we let the absurd incidents soak in. There were just surprises left and right. I firmly believe our carefree attitude led to these unbelievable incidents. Because we left ourselves open for anything, anything could happen. Sounds simple, but it worked.

We rarely turned any opportunity down that others would face with caution. I continued that search for something more. Jackson and I were shocked when we entered the coffee shop.

When I had entered the other coffee shop on the first day, it was playing reggae music. This coffee shop was playing Notorious B.I.G. This was underground stuff that we had never heard before. We bought more weed, and I rolled another joint. Jackson and I sat in a booth, toked, and listened.

The bass was loud and we heard, "Here I am, I'll be damned if this ain't some shit. Come to spread the butter lyrics over hominy grit."

———————————

Jackson and I decided we would enjoy the park the next day, and we headed back to the Flying Pig. We went up to the room for more rest, and we came across two American guys about our age. They were Yankees to a tee.

One was short, kind of chunky, with a black goatee. He was sporting jeans, a funky T-shirt, and a Mets hat. He was much more forthcoming than his partner in crime. American number two was slightly taller, skinny, and very quiet.

As we entered the room, the bigger one called out, "Hey youse guys, what's your names?"

I had this deep-down disdain for northerners. Being from the South, we still believed the Civil War was not over. Enjoying a slower pace of life and speaking with a drawl were all pluses in my book. There was no substitution for southern hospitality. Being stuck in the machine of the North just didn't make sense to me. Maybe I was naïve, but cutting another guy off at the knees to make a buck was not my cup of tea. And who doesn't drink sweet tea?

Granted, I was young, but the narrow-mindedness of my upbringing was deeply embedded. I mustered enough resistance to my natural instincts and gave these two individuals a chance. Sort of.

"My name is Cam and this here is Jackson," I said back to him in a strong Southern accent.

"Oh yeah? My name is Ross. This is Chuck. We're from New York City. I can tell youse guys is from the South. You like the Braves?"

His Mets hat screamed obnoxious fan, but I couldn't abandon my beloved Atlanta Braves. I thought I'd get a jeer out. I spoke in a strong twang to start the friendly banter. Reinforcing the stereotype on my side was only fair.

"Hell yeah, I like the Braves. Ain't you tired of that country ass whoopin' they give y'all every year?"

"Man, we fucking hate the Braves. That Chipper Jones is a chotch."

"Chipper is a damn legend, son." I wished I had a dip in to spit for emphasis. "He just a good ol' redneck with a knack for tossin' the cueball around the yard. Secret's in the dirt. I reckon this ain't gone be no argument worth fightin' over."

"So I'm high as balls," Jackson interrupted.

There was an awkward moment of silence and then some laughing. The Yankees were stoned too.

"Well, we goin' yonder after supper to check out them hussies in the Red Light District. Heard you can't come here without at least seeing it," I said in midlaugh. "Girl, show me that squirrel! Know what I mean, Ross?"

I slapped him on the butt just to freak him out.

"Oh yeah. There's some hot cakes over there," Ross said.

I responded quickly under my breath, "Like the bulldogs up North, I'm sure."

Jackson heard me and giggled.

Before Yankee Doodle caught on, I quickly continued, "Well, you gentlemen are more than welcome to join us."

Being sarcastic was always my specialty, and I really liked to see how far I could take it. I basically had a terrible habit of lying, but I justified it as imaginative conversation.

My favorite conversations occurred when meeting someone for the first time. Gullible people were so much fun to mess with. I never truthfully engaged in the initial topics of hometown, major, job, and the God-forbidden name-dropping game. I focused on more implausible and questionable situations. I just conveyed them with such seriousness; the other party couldn't help but believe me or get really confused.

One of my favorite personas was a partying, jet-cruising Canadian plumber. I used this personality multiple times with girls when going to the beach during college. Meeting someone new at a party usually included a boring conversation. When asked what I did, I'd say I was a plumber from Canada and just flew in for the party.

People's initial reaction tells a lot about their personality and level of acceptance. Some would frown and look down on me with disdain.

Others would get thoroughly confused, and I enjoyed my own internal laughter because that person was soaking in my complete bullshit.

I would continue that I had a flight at two in the morning to get back to work on Sunday. Sometimes I would tell them I set a record for the company by unclogging twenty-four toilets in twenty-four hours. Then, I'd just end the conversation and go back to my friends like nothing happened.

Other times, I'd say my name was Bubba, and I just got out of prison. If I was holding a can of beer, I would claim that I would never drink from a bottle again; too many bad memories. I'd say I didn't believe in bars of soap anymore either. Part of my rehabilitation was to read Bingo numbers at the elderly homes; I had seen many decrepit people jump out of their wheelchairs to claim their winnings.

Sometimes I claimed to be an interpretive dance instructor for blind kids. I would show some emotion, claiming that I loved those little buggers. I'd say I majored in basket weaving in college but I developed a cocaine problem because I needed to stay up all night to complete the weaving in time.

I'm not really sure why I got such pleasure out of doing this. Maybe the truth just wasn't exciting enough for me.

Every once in a while, there would be someone quick enough to catch on. They would play along, and it made for an inside joke that we could both share. One time I told a girl I was a big black man named Tyrone. She pretended she was an Asian named Victoria. The night turned out well.

In between the sheets, I would say, "Tyrone needs some sugar."

Creepy? Possibly. Memorable? Absolutely. I guess she always fantasized about being with a big black man. Most of the time, I never really got around to telling the truth. It was a good way to weed through the ordinary folks, and people always seemed to remember me the next time I saw them. Regardless of the thrills and memories these untruthful escapades brought, I hadn't fully developed a conscience and vaguely understood the concept of conviction. Inevitably, time would take care of that.

The Red Light District was within a couple of miles of the hostel, and the four of us walked toward it with anticipation. I didn't plan on paying for anything, just sightseeing. Soon, we were close to the narrow alley. As we walked through the crowd, there was window after window of risqué women. Some were wearing lingerie, some titties were out, and many of the prostitutes were moving provocatively, motioning us to come inside. I couldn't help but notice how beautiful some of the women were. But there was this strange dynamic involved while looking in the windows.

The prostitutes seemed like living mannequins. It was literally shopping for human beings. I can't deny that the thought of going inside crossed my mind. Somehow, my moral compass steered me away from the allure of prepaid sex. The people I was with helped me make the decision to stay at a distance.

There were dirty old Middle Eastern men standing outside looking as well. I couldn't fathom the thought of checking under the hood when many people had already used their own dipstick. Jackson had a little harder time resisting.

Jackson's hormones were rampant, and he claimed, "I want to go in there and get some."

"Man, you don't want to do that. They are hot, but you are just paying for sex. Something is wrong with that."

"Come on, man. It will just be once."

"No way. You can do so much better than that," I said.

I somehow felt it was degrading to even attempt to engage in such an activity. Even under my egotism, I had empathy for the girls in the window. How could they put themselves through that? I couldn't figure out the deeper things I struggled with, but the prostitutes' dilemma screamed dysfunction and pain. There was no self-respect, and I couldn't fathom supplementing their downward spiral.

Yes, they were making a living, but it just didn't make sense. It was fun to look at it, but it soon became disgraceful. It fed into every carnal temptation, and I somehow resisted and put up a roadblock for Jackson as well. I looked, but I didn't touch.

The New Yorkers didn't engage in any sexual activity either. The four of us spent the next few minutes completing the route, and then we made our way to another part of town.

We collectively decided to partake in another vice common to all of us, smoking ourselves into oblivion. Ross was a self-proclaimed weed expert, and we all found yet another coffee shop to waste our time.

We entered, and Ross already had his variations of grass on him. Sitting in a booth, he broke up four different strands and put it all into one large joint. We passed the eclectic doobie around and managed to finish half of it. I got obliterated. Neither Jackson nor I could complete the activity. That was the highest I had been in my whole life. It was uncomfortable and nauseating.

When you reach the maximum of being stoned, it becomes mundane. At that point, I actually made a semi-declaration to quit smoking. I would not follow through with my promise, but my mind throbbed with apathy and unproductive thought. The experience was what I had looked forward to since planning the trip, but the moment was just too intense.

Somehow, I was able to regroup after about thirty minutes. Then, the munchies kicked in. It was time to find food and quick. Being high as a treetop made anything seem delicious. My senses were so heightened that the simple act of salivating produced euphoria.

After leaving the coffee shop, I found a hamburger stand that also sold French fries. I bought a burger and eagerly dumped mayonnaise all over the French fries. It was a European tradition, and it really hit the spot. I think a piece of cardboard with salt and pepper would have tasted delicious too.

We spent the rest of the night at the Flying Pig. The bar was not crowded, and our rooms were just up the stairs. Jackson and I ditched the Yankees, and we sat at the bar enjoying a few beers. We drank several rounds and talked about things that didn't make sense but seemed to be insightful.

Jackson and I had some hash, so we decided to make our way to the pillow-filled lounge and continue smoking that instead of our weed. This was not my first time dealing with hash.

As a freshman, I was at the bottom of the fraternity's totem poll. Pledging was demeaning, and my class had to prove our worth for the majority of the year. The peer pressure from the older brothers was strong, but the division did create unity within my class.

The idea of partaking in demeaning activities to join a group may seem strange to some, but a sense of camaraderie and loyalty developed among my peers.

Pledging lasted through Thanksgiving, and everyone was anxious for Christmas break. By January, we were officially brothers. Some of the older guys eased up and became friendly. Others remained assholes.

During the spring, we had to prepare for our formal. Most fraternities took off to another location like Charleston to rent hotel rooms or beach houses. We did it a little differently, which I liked a lot. We had our formal at our house, which was much more fun with much less liability. For other houses' formals, there were always stories of restrictions from hotels and run-ins with the law.

The theme of our formal was an island party, and it required a tremendous effort by all classes. The freshmen were required to bring massive amounts of bamboo. The bamboo had to be at least as thick as a Coke can and over twenty-four feet tall. The rest of the older classes built the hut from within two large wedding tents. There was a thirty-foot slide to enter the hut. We weren't allowed to see the finished product until the night of the party.

First, we had to rent the biggest U-Haul we could find. Two friends and I went to go rent the truck from Raleigh. Raleigh was a hometown for one of them, but he lacked a good amount of common sense.

At the rental office, I showed a fake ID in order to rent the truck. The employee just needed someone to be twenty-one, and my ID showed that I was over the age. Whatever works, I guess.

Well, my pledge brother, lacking common sense, directed me through downtown Raleigh to begin the trip back to Chapel Hill. I had never driven a truck that big, Raleigh had a lot of one-way streets, and it was a challenge to say the least. To this day, I have an appreciation for those who can drive a true big rig.

After getting a good feel for how to drive the truck, the pledge class took turns making the one hundred mile trip east to gather from a large bamboo forest. During one particular trip, Gator, another friend, Johnny, and I took off early in the morning.

Gator, in good fashion, had come across some hash. I volunteered to drive, and we packed a bowl of hash and smoked it down the highways of eastern North Carolina. I had some hesitancy, but I pushed discretion aside. They sat back and enjoyed the ride; I got in the zone and gripped the wheel all the way there.

The radio was nothing special, but Guess Who's "American Woman" came on, enticing us to play it at full blast. The minute it came on, we passed an American flag waving in a front yard, and the song ended as we passed by another American flag. This may seem mundane; but as we rode across rural lands, my thoughts floated into deep reflection.

Taking in the surroundings in such an altered state felt like insight into the inner workings of the American lifestyle. We rode past poor homes and tobacco fields. There was a flash into the past of a surreal combination of how hard people worked and a temptation to run away from the challenge. When the song ended, I asked Gator and Johnny if they had seen what I did, and they just nodded. It seemed like too deep of a topic to discuss out loud.

Each time I got high, I came across a regular situation with strong analysis, sometimes too strong. When diving into the depths of experience, I felt like I was more enlightened than during everyday life. I kept expanding my mind in order to gain better insight. There were definitely memorable experiences, but they were skewed.

Those thoughts and beliefs I developed in my drug-filled state only made sense as I continued to live in that kind of haze. Some people may disagree, but your brain regulates itself if you rid yourself of drugs for a long enough time. I was nowhere near this belief system at that time in my life, and I fully endorsed drugs and the pleasure obtained.

Jackson and I stayed downstairs all night and went back and forth from the smoking lounge to the hostel bar until it closed. Before going to sleep, we stared out the window at the sunrise. It was a touching moment, but Jackson eliminated all of the sentimentality.

There was an old slice of half-eaten pizza sitting on the window ledge. I guess he was hungry, and he just reached over and started eating it. I don't think he thought about the pizza's age or decay. I was mesmerized by the view of the sunrise, but then I saw Jackson taking a bite out of the corner of my eye. I didn't say anything right away.

I waited a couple of moments, and then I asked, "Hey man, where did you get that pizza?"

Jackson paused and stared out the window with extreme concentration; he said slowly, "I don't know man . . . I don't know."

After delayed cognition, we burst into one of the strongest episodes of laughter I have ever had. We laughed for what seemed like eternity. Tears streamed down our faces, and every time we looked back at each other, we continued to lose it. Once we finally calmed down, we entered our room. I lay down, continued to laugh, and fell asleep.

8

The no-agenda plan was working out perfectly. I woke up when I was absolutely ready. Today, the mission was to visit the Heineken factory. This was our last day in Amsterdam, and we wanted to make the most of it. Supposedly, we just had to pay an entrance fee, and we'd be able to drink as many samples as we wanted. That seemed like a good plan to the both of us.

Jackson and I readied ourselves for the day and walked out of the Flying Pig. The weather was perfect, and the walk was pleasant. We reached a bridge going over one of the canals, and the enormous sign for Heineken rested on top of a large building at a distance. We kept going but when we got to the door, the factory was closed. It was a tremendous disappointment, but the situation turned out better than expected.

It was lunchtime, and there was small café next to the factory. Jackson and I took a seat outside. The front of the building was wide open, and a man sat inside sipping a beer in a unique glass.

"Excuse me, sir. What kind of beer is that?" I asked.

The man looked up and said, "This is a Belgian beer called La Chouffe. Give it a try."

When the waitress came over, Jackson and I ordered two La Chouffes. She came back quickly with two curved glasses full of blonde beer with a strong head. There was a small leprechaun turned diagonally on the glass.

The waitress said, "You'll know you've had too many when the little man starts dancing."

Jackson and I laughed, and we really thought she was only kidding. As we got halfway through the beer, we realized she was not. As I finished mine off, I had quite a strong buzz. Jackson talked normally, and then he said something to me that just seemed to stick.

"You always finish your beer before I do," Jackson declared.

"What? I guess I'm just bigger than you are; I need more to drink," I said with some justification.

I was proud of the fact that I could drink so much, but Jackson had a tone of concern in his voice. I brushed him off, but the comment has stuck with me ever since. Instead of listening, I wanted to prove him wrong.

At the café, we ate an awesome cheeseburger topped with a fried egg and drank another glass of La Chouffe. The little man was definitely dancing. He was actually boogying by then. An idea popped into my head, facilitated by my inebriation.

In a low voice, I whispered, "All right Jackson, we are going to buy some mushrooms. We'll save them for the right time during the trip."

Like anyone in Amsterdam would have been surprised by the plan.

Jackson shrugged his shoulders and simply said, "All right."

Amsterdam was losing its luster. I had been walking around stoned for three days. I reached a point where I was so high that it seemed like I wasn't high at all. It was a strange feeling. The coffee shop scene was getting repetitive, but we continued to go in them and waste the day. This time, I purchased some mushrooms and put them away for a better day.

Even though it was early in the three-week trip, we missed the South. To cover up any fear of being in such a foreign place, we went to a liquor store and bought a fifth of Four Roses bourbon. The store was quaint, and we realized this was a good chance to obtain the coveted absinthe as well.

There were bottles of the bright green substance, and we found the most expensive one. The cashier put our two bottles in a bag, and we made our way out the door. We decided to save the absinthe for special occasions as well.

The park we had passed the day before was less crowded so we went in and found a tree to sit under. Without regard, I cracked open the bottle of bourbon and took a pull. It was early afternoon.

We just sat there the rest of the day and sipped on the familiar liquor. The day grew to evening, and we made our way back to the hostel once again. When we entered, we saw two beautiful dark-haired girls with golden brown skin.

Instead of roaming the streets, Jackson and I decided to stick around the hostel for the night, mainly enamored by these two gorgeous girls. The immense amount of marijuana over the past days was starting to take its toll.

Jackson actually took the reins on getting this encounter started. He found out these two sexy girls were from Argentina. We ate sandwiches from the bar with them, and then the four of us went to the basement, which we did not know existed. This bottom floor was somewhat of an extension of the lounge, and it had plenty of places to sit and relax. We brought the rest of our bourbon with us.

We sat with the two girls and talked about everything. One had a guitar with her, and she was not shy. As she played, the Spanish words in each song rolled off her tongue, and it was very peaceful and satisfying. Other people came in and out, but for the most part, it was just the four of us.

Jackson and I were getting back to our roots, and we personified the typical good ol' boys. We drank our bourbon, danced, and clapped along to the tunes.

Later in the night, we noticed a tall skinny German. We invited him to sit at our table for a short while. We offered him a pull of bourbon, and he took it, not without consequences. He cringed and gasped, amazed that Jackson and I could drink it straight from the bottle.

Over in the corner, a middle-aged man was sitting by himself on a sofa. I wanted to make friends so I sat next to him and started chatting. I actually responded truthfully to his questions for a change. He was from Spain. As we spoke, my joyous frame of mind shifted suddenly. The somber man's voice throbbed with heartache and despair. He smiled as he spoke, but his eyes were full of tears.

At that point, I made my decision about Amsterdam. The freedom was too much, and a full picture was being painted as I gazed around the room. The lack of rules enabled people to give in to a darker part of themselves. The lack of restrictions would shape the style of the painting I would construct. Much like the paintings I had seen in the Van Gogh museum, the canvas would hold an image that was slightly skewed. There was a visible scene in each of Van Gogh's paintings, but it was mostly a combination of erratic paint strokes that are marvelously placed into a congruent image. Van Gogh's work was brilliant no doubt, but he is also the guy who cut his ear off to send to his girlfriend. In his life, there was a struggle to maintain his sanity while also preserving his talent. Van Gogh managed to find an outlet for the ups and downs he went through that others could appreciate. Deep down, I aspired to do the same.

These Argentineans had vibrant souls and the passion of youth. They exuded a natural happiness as well as a cultural divide that made them stand out on my imaginary canvas. They were one of the few bright colors on my imaginary palette, and their presence made an outline of the picture I would paint.

The German was introverted. As we spoke with him, we learned that he had a dysfunctional relationship with his father. His color was darker, and he looked like a weary traveler. He represented the dwindling color as the painting moved toward its central point.

The Spanish man embodied the majority of the painting I wanted to create. His sad eyes, which he tried to hide, were in the middle of the canvas, surrounded by spiraling color. His attempt to escape his life was very apparent. His eyes were the dullest color in the image.

I saw the whole painted canvas as individual colors that blended together and continually spiraled outward from dark to light. This is how I viewed Amsterdam. It was dual edged. The city was either a murky place where you spiraled downward to escape reality or a place of endurance as you made your way toward the outside of the painting where there were lighter colors. The pull inward was stronger than the projection outward.

I was an observer, I didn't like my realization, and I was ready to leave. I could not muster enough energy to pursue one of the Argentineans. We finished the bottle of bourbon, and the night faded away.

In our vague plan to travel Europe, our next stop was Geneva, Switzerland. Initially, I thought that we would go back to Munich and then ride over to Geneva. Before we left Amsterdam, I went online to book the train tickets, but the original route didn't make sense.

Jackson and I would have to go over the Alps, and it would be much easier to just cut through France. We had a night to spare before the music festival started, and visiting Paris seemed ideal. The key words there were "seemed ideal."

Our train to Paris left at ten o'clock that morning. We woke up in plenty of time. I had forgotten about the disappointment of the previous night. Today was a new day, and we could still smoke weed legally. I stashed some in my backpack to save for the rest of the trip. Before officially checking out, we took bong rips in the smoking lounge, which eliminated any sense of a hangover. The train station was a block away, and we were right on schedule.

As we exhaled the rest of the smoke, we realized we had not bought any souvenirs (other than drugs). There were some specialty shops on the way to the station.

We entered a tourist shop. I wanted a soccer T-shirt. Ajax, the professional soccer club of Amsterdam, had a really cool logo, a side view of a bearded man's face with an extended head full of intertwined symbols of the city. Unfortunately, I was far too high and accidentally bought an extra small. Shucks.

Before getting to the train station, we made one final stop at a coffee shop. Instead of smoking, we bought space cakes, brownies prepared by using THC oil. Right outside the train station, we took turns taking pictures of each other eating the delightful treat. Our cheeks were full, but only we would know what they were filled with.

Jackson and I ate the brownies quickly, and at first we didn't feel anything. We checked in at the station, got on the train, and headed for Paris. Then things started to get funky.

Instead of sitting side by side, Jackson and I took seats facing each other. As the moments passed, our body high increased. Whatever was in the brownies was very potent. This was not like an ordinary, subtle high; it was an absolute roller coaster.

As the train traveled to Paris at top speed, it went into and out of a variety of tunnels. The dancing lights of the daylight and the opposing darkness of the tunnels were tripping me and Jackson out big time. It felt like we were in the water tunnel in Willy Wonka. Imaginary images flashed on the walls of the tunnels.

We yelled and gasped like children. We were right in the middle of a crowded train car, and we were losing our minds. The other passengers stared at us, but no one spoke. We probably weren't the first people to leave the Amsterdam train station under the influence.

The psychedelic adventure continued for a good thirty to forty-five minutes. It finally waned, and Jackson and I regained our composure. As we talked about the roller coaster ride, we kept repeating, "Dude," "Man," and "Whoa." Other words didn't fit in appropriately.

About an hour into the trip, the complete experience of Amsterdam finally sank in. We were exhausted, and sleep came into the picture once again. Jackson and I passed out, much to the relief of the other passengers.

The train ride, which was only supposed to last three and a half hours, took eight. While we were sleeping, part of the train track was blocked by a fire. The train came to a halt, and it sat there until the fires were extinguished.

When Jackson and I woke up, all we could do was wait out the ride. Boredom set in quickly. Only so many thoughts can pass through during such a time. Conversation between me and Jackson was boring, and we were comfortable enough with each other to sit in silence. Eventually we became aggravated, and the other passengers murmured complaints as the hours drew on. There was nothing anybody on the train could do but wait.

After an agonizing trip, we arrived in Paris. The idea of Paris seemed wonderful, but practicality caught up to the notion. First, we had a little scare.

Since we were entering another country, we had to pass through customs, just as if we were in an airport. Jackson had his bag of weed in his pocket.

When I remembered his stash, I asked him quickly, "Jackson, do you still have that weed in your pocket?"

The realization hit him as well as he said, "Holy shit, yeah."

"Throw that shit away. We do not want to go to jail in Europe."

"Damn it. All right."

As Jackson exited the train, he reached in his pocket and slid the bag into the trash. I could see his thought process and accompanying emotions the whole way. It was written all over his face. His mood shifted dramatically from worry and contemplation to relief and then to disappointment.

I reassured him, "I've got some tucked away in my bag. It's not much, but it should do."

After passing through customs, Jackson and I grabbed a bite to eat, and then we walked down the street, carrying our backpacks. We didn't realize that June was the high season for Paris, and almost every hotel and hostel had been booked for weeks.

We must have tried ten places looking for a room, all of which were completely full. We had been walking for miles, and it was getting late. We debated our next move.

"This is fucking terrible," I whined.

"No kidding," Jackson agreed.

"Look, there is a park over there. If this next hotel doesn't work out, let's just bite the bullet and sleep there."

"We'll probably get robbed, Cam. Let's keep trying."

"All right, deal."

As we were walking, we saw a nice hotel to our left. There were some teenage girls hanging out on the balcony.

One of the girls yelled down to us, "Hey! Are you guys backpacking?"

We both had huge backpacks on, so this question was completely rhetorical, but I saw the potential so I engaged with them. They looked like impressionable high school girls, and I hoped to intrigue them with our adventure.

"Sure are," I said proudly. "We have been all across Europe. What are you girls doing up there?"

Another girl chirped, "Wow, backpacking sounds so cool! We are on a high school trip from Texas."

Continuing to swindle them, I said, "Well, listen, girls. Me and my buddy need a place to sleep. How about if we come up there to sleep on the floor? We'll be out of the room early tomorrow morning."

As we continued to propose the idea to these girls, this dickweed kid interrupted.

This punk yelled from the adjoining balcony, "You guys need some money?"

As he spoke, he threw a Euro coin down at us. We were thoroughly insulted, and Jackson's Irish temper took over.

He screamed up to where the kid was standing, "Listen, motherfucker! I don't need any goddamn money. Shut the hell up and go back inside."

The girls' eyes lit up, and the display of male bravado convinced them to let us come up. Jackson and I felt a little creepy, but we were desperate for a place to sleep.

We entered the lobby, and the concierge completely ruined our plan. We didn't look particularly clean or presentable, and he wouldn't allow us to use the elevator. The stereotype is true: the French are assholes.

There was nothing we could really do but leave and move on. As we left, the girls asked where we were going, and we just told them we were going to sleep in the park. Much more adventurous.

Jackson and I walked down the street, but we still resisted sleeping in the park. We lowered our standards and tried one more place several blocks away. This was a deteriorated part of town, and the white building had chipped paint and a broken window.

I entered first, and the worn and dingy red carpet reeked of mildew. The light was dim from the overhead chandelier. There was no one in the front room.

I yelled, "Bonjour!" and a small French man walked down the short staircase to approach us.

He didn't speak any English; we didn't speak any French.

After beating our heads against the language barrier, I grabbed a piece of paper and drew a room with a bed in it. Next to it, I sketched a dollar sign and put a question mark. I handed the paper to him, and he wrote down 35. We were satisfied and paid him promptly.

He grabbed a set of keys, and we followed him up the staircase. The hallway was narrow, and there were several couples in other rooms. Something was not quite right about the situation. We smelled cigarettes and saw several women wearing lingerie in open rooms. Jackson and I were just looking for a place to sleep.

We reached the door to our room, the small man wiggled the key, and the door swung open. It was pitiful. There was a sink to the left, an old wooden television, and a single bed in the corner. The man danced around the room, turning the water on and off and patting the pillow. I nodded just to get him to leave the room. There was no air conditioning, and Jackson and I had been sweating for hours.

"All right, sweet," Jackson proclaimed sarcastically.

I responded, "This is what's going to happen: We are going to share that bed, sleep back to back, and forget this ever happened."

I stripped down to my boxers, and Jackson did the same. It was like a sauna. I washed my face with some semi-cool water and laid down facing the wall. We did not go to bed happy.

9

Jackson and I woke up early and hopped out of bed. This was not what we expected, and we were ready to get to Geneva.

"Let's get the hell out of here," I commanded.

Jackson didn't have to say anything. He just nodded, and we made our way out of that nasty place and headed toward the train station as quickly as possible. We learned later that the Cathedral of Notre Dame was only a block away. We were in such a bad mood, we didn't even care. Our main focus was to get on our way to Geneva. The music festival was starting the next day, another anticipated event in the trip.

Jackson and I took our seats on the train and prayed for an uninterrupted trip. We let the dust settle, and I had to say something about the night before. It was against my plan to forget, but I needed some kind of affirmation of where we had slept.

"Jackson, did you notice anything strange about that place last night?" I questioned.

"Other than us avoiding a midnight swordfight in a single bed, not really. Why?"

"Man, I think that was a whorehouse. Did you see the women in the other rooms?"

"No way. There is no way."

I had not showered in at least two days, and I felt like garbage. After much debate, we concluded that it had been a whorehouse. Neither of us could deny that we slept where many had slept before. My stomach churned in disgust. It could have been something to laugh about, but I just wasn't in the mood. I could not believe it.

As we approached Geneva, we could see the snowcapped Alps. It was almost the middle of the summer, but the mountaintops stayed white all year long. I was impressed by the terrain and looked forward to exploring this city, especially with a music festival going on. This was not my first music festival either.

Most seniors in high school take a trip to the beach or a cruise for graduation. In June of 2005, four of my friends from high school decided to do it a little differently. We decided to go to the Bonaroo music festival in Manchester, Tennessee.

Before tickets were available, the five of us waited anxiously for the weekend passes to go on sale. The festival had been going on for about five years, and it drew over one hundred thousand people each year. We thought the tickets would sell out immediately. We went online and bought five tickets for $180 each. This ticket included an all weekend pass to some of the best music around.

Transportation was a key element of the trip. Our friend Scott's dad had the perfect vehicle: a 1970s Scooby Doo green Volkswagen van. It screamed hippie, and we thought that was so cool. The van had a yellow and green plaid interior, a working oven and stovetop, a couch in the back, and an expandable camper roof with a bed up top.

It had been sitting under Scott's car port for quite some time, and we gave it a full wash before we headed to Manchester. We took the Green Machine to a mechanic, and everything seemed to be in good condition.

I had learned how to drive a stick before I got my license. Jackson and I would actually steal his older sister's car when we were fourteen and go get Krystal burgers. When I taught him how to drive the Honda Accord, he stalled out so bad that the trunk popped open.

Scott also knew how to drive a stick, and we planned that he would drive up and I would drive back. We also packed a Ford Expedition full of supplies, and the five of us were ready to go.

On a Thursday afternoon, we revved the engines and headed west up I-20 toward Atlanta. About an hour into the trip, we ran into our first problem.

Scott was driving the van, and I was sitting in the back with our pal Eric. Eric was the party guy. Not necessarily a huge partier personally, he was always hosting high school bashes. His parents loved to travel, and they left the house to Eric frequently. Eric also had several properties around Ellington including a lake house and two farms.

One time, Eric's Dad was going to China for three weeks and we decided that we were going to have the biggest party of the year at his farm.

This farm had a huge garage with a built-in stage. It was perfect for a band. We called it Ericpalooza. Somehow, we managed to get two kegs, and there were well over a hundred people in attendance. It was mighty impressive for a high school party.

The place was rural, but one of the neighbors was close enough to call the cops. When the cop first pulled up, most everybody went running into the woods. The band kept playing, and Jackson was the only one still dancing in front of them. Another example of Jackson's inattentiveness and laissez-faire attitude. Since this party was in a backward county as well, the cop rolled up, told us to be quiet, and left. But I diverge from my story of our original musical conquest. Long story short, we all liked Eric. He was super guy.

Well, Eric and I were sitting in the back of the van while Scott drove. Cruising along the interstate at the van's maximum speed of sixty-five miles per hour, I wanted to get high. Yes, we had prepared by bringing adequate amounts. Just as I put some weed in a bowl and reached for the lighter, the car started to lean toward the back left. One of the tires had gone flat.

We put the weed back away and figured it would only take a minute to change the tire. Eric took full control, and he grabbed the tools and the spare tire. He began to change it, and the rest of us made conversation on the side of the interstate. After some small talk, a cop pulled up to help us out.

Seeing a policeman was not a pleasant sight. We were underage with drugs and alcohol in the car. Driving a VW van was like having a Phish sticker on your car. The cops know what's going on. I jumped inside the van and hid the weed deep in our luggage. The cop was curious.

"Well, boys. You having a little car trouble?" the man in uniform asked.

Scott piped up, "Just a little tire change. No big deal really."

"That's an interesting van you got there. Where y'all heading?"

I knew how fragile our image was so I lied. "We are going to see some relatives in Tennessee."

"Oh, I see." The cop's radio beeped and a frazzled voice came out. "Hey Charlie! You see them hippie boys? Heard they got a flat."

The cop grabbed his radio, clicked the button, and responded, "Yeah, Bob. Right here with them. Come over and check it out."

I usually played things cool, but I was pretty distraught inside. The second cop car pulled up on the side of the road. If they found a reason to search either car, we were fucked. All of us tried to keep a calm demeanor.

Eric worked feverishly to change the tire on the hot Georgia asphalt. As it turned out, the cops were actually very laid back, and we made friends quickly. As Eric tightened down the last nut, I asked the cop for a picture.

"Sir, can we get a picture with you in front of your car?" I asked politely.

"I'm afraid I can't do that. Turns out, y'all have been on camera the whole time. Got one sitting on the dashboard. Tell you what. I'll take one of y'all."

The five of us stepped in front of his Greene County cop car and got our first picture for the trip. It was a pretty funny scene. We all shook hands with the two cops and got back into the van to leave.

That spare tire wasn't going to make it all the way to Tennessee, so we needed to find a mechanic somewhere. Like a miracle, when we took the next exit, there was a huge tire store. This was really the middle of nowhere, and there was the full service tire center.

The five of us figured we just needed to replace one tire, and we could pitch in fifteen or twenty bucks apiece. Unbeknownst to us, all the tires on that old van were dry-rotted. It needed four new tires. When Scott had taken it to the mechanic back in Ellington, the idiot forgot to check the tires.

All of us turned to Eric and begged him to use his credit card. He agreed, and we left the van at the tire shop and walked next door to a Zaxby's to eat.

After about an hour, we were back on the road. Eric and I started smoking, and I ate a whole pan of brownies that his mom had made. It was quite strange as we got closer to the festival. There had to be a ten-mile radius of hippies. They were everywhere. We saw people with dreadlocks and tie-dye shirts at every gas station, on the side of the road, and in other cars. The interstate was packed so we took some back roads.

Somehow those back roads took us right into the Bonaroo property. Since we were in such a cool van, we were let right into the line with an accompanying peace sign.

When we pulled up in the field, it was pretty frantic. Cars were lined up, and people started setting up camping gear, tables, and chairs. Everyone made some attempt to mark their territory and set up some area suitable for the weekend. We got lucky with that.

A small Acura pulled in between our two vehicles. We had a tarp, and we strung it up from the top of the camper across to the Expedition. After placing a table and chairs in the middle, we had an outdoor living room of some sort.

Our neighbor liked music, but he was obviously there on business. He had driven in from Missouri, and we greeted him once everything was settled. He grabbed a tackle box out of his car, and each compartment had a different type of weed in it. This guy was looking to do some heavy-duty selling.

Security for the festival was completely lax. The only rule was against bringing in glass bottles. Some security people rode around on horses, but that was it. We stayed up late the first night and prepared for the next day of music.

The first band we saw was Old Crow Medicine Show. They sang the song "Take 'em Away," and I was hooked. The second-to-last chorus just hit me:

Land that I love is the land that I'm workin'
But it's hard to love it all the time when your back is a-hurtin'
Gettin' too old now to push this here plow
Please let me lay down so I can look at the clouds.

I hadn't farmed a day in my life, but I liked the words in that song. Why was everybody around me working so hard? I mean, what was the ultimate goal of constantly striving for success? Granted, these verses were talking about a man who had worked the land all of his life, but this was another internal dilemma I was in. Always extremely motivated to achieve, I also wanted to just relax. Somewhat of a perfectionist, I never really allowed myself to completely enjoy the lighter things of life.

Escaping the responsibilities of growing up by partying was probably what balanced me out for the time being. It ended up being a hard balance to maintain for an extended amount of time. It was similar to holding a bowling ball in each hand. Eventually, I was going to drop one.

Nevertheless, the crowd roared when the song ended, and I knew the party had begun. This time in my life was comparable to the trip to Europe. We got all drugged up and drunk, but nothing too intense. We really did hear some great music, and it was an awesome trip. However, it was a little different because of the crowd.

Before going to Manchester, I thought the music scene was the titties. I had an eclectic selection of music. I burned CDs very early on, and I always wanted to have just the right song for any situation. Yeah, I know; it is a little OCD. I wasn't a snob about music; I just liked listening to it. I didn't have any musical talent either, so I made up for it by having good taste in what I listened to.

After spending three days without bathing, I came to the conclusion that hippies were worthless. This was confirmed by the end of the trip. Our sketchy neighbor brought back the first piece of evidence.

On the second day, I was taking a nap in the top of the Green Machine. The Wheelin' Dealin' Missourian was sitting in our outdoor "living room" with a middle-aged man wearing hippie clothes and a cap with a multicolored mushroom stitched on it. Their conversation woke me up.

"Man, I've been traveling across the country for this stuff, man," the man said. "I started in San Diego with my motorcycle. It broke down in Arizona, so I just left it on the side of the road, man. I bought a bus ticket to Nashville, and I hitchhiked from there."

"That's cool, man," our neighbor said.

Actually, that's not cool, man. You are not one of the characters in Easy Rider, the sixties are over, and you are hanging out with a bunch of eighteen-year-olds.

The creepy hippie packed a metal pipe full of something, reached in a plastic bag, and sprinkled some substance on top. He lit the pipe and went into another world. Old Man River passed it to Mastermind Missouri, and he took a hit. My friends refused to smoke whatever was in that pipe. The old man saw me peering through the screen up top and asked if I wanted to hit it. I just said no and lay back down.

The second incident happened on the way out that Sunday. A grungy, long-haired hippie was sitting on the road with a sign that just said, "Next stop, Wakarusa." That festival was in Arkansas. That piece of shit had probably been traveling around the country for years, going to festivals, and mooching off anything he could. The combination of the aged man doing drugs with teenagers and this guy with the sign helped me come to my quick judgment that hippies were not the symbol of a positive contribution to society. Not being a liberal didn't help my conclusions either.

All in all, it was a great trip, but I had not been to a music festival since. The one in Geneva included thirty stages set up throughout the city. There was music from all over the world including jazz, orchestras, rock, and cover bands. I was pumped. Plus, my birthday was right around the corner.

10

We reached our hostel in Geneva, and I had a sudden realization. Neither Jackson nor I had called home to let our mothers know that we found each other. It had been four days since I had called. Little did we know what had transpired in Ellington. Jackson and I really didn't find out until we got back from the trip.

I called my mom to let her know we were alive, and Jackson called his mom to explain the situation. Short calls on both parts, and we got back into vacation mode. Big underestimation of the drama going on Stateside.

Apparently, everybody in Ellington had heard that Jackson was missing. Rumors spread like wildfire. People thought he had been kidnapped or killed, or he was wandering in some European country with an unpronounceable name.

After I got off of the phone that first day in Amsterdam, Mrs. McKinley had called Dr. Traugott immediately. They checked the hospitals and called the police in Munich. They came to the apartment and banged on the door while Jackson was asleep. People were praying for him at church. His mom was about to send in his photo to CNN to report a missing person.

The reaction from the people our age was the funniest. Our trip was of great interest to those who couldn't go. Jackson's older sister was at a popular Ellington bar one night after Jackson had been proclaimed missing. She was wasted, and she stopped the band and got on stage in tears to make an announcement. She asked everybody to help her find her brother. Jackson and I were just stoned in Amsterdam while all of this was going down. Jackson caught hell when he got back to Ellington, and people still bring it up today.

Before returning to Munich, we stayed another day in Geneva. We explored the city, a very cool place. We went to a famous cathedral and climbed up to the top. The tiles on the roof made a really interesting and colorful pattern.

Scaffolding surrounded the highest part of the church. I have a fear of heights and clung to the walls of the church because of the unsteady structure. I swear it was moving with the wind. It did reveal an awesome view of the city, running down to the crystal-clear waters of Lake Geneva.

We also went to the park that held the Reformation Wall. Switzerland had been the middle ground during the changing religious doctrines of the seventeenth century, and there was a tribute on the grounds of the University of Geneva. There are four huge statues of William Farel, John Calvin, Theodore Beza, and John Knox, who were all influential in some aspect. Jackson and I didn't really know their historical significance; we just thought it was a cool place for a picture. The statues had to be thirty-five feet tall.

The hangover from Amsterdam was still looming, so we took it easy that night. Jackson and I checked into the City Hostel Geneva. It was not as interesting as the Flying Pig, but it was just fine with for sleeping. Plus, it was much better than sharing a single bed in a whore house. Instead of going out, we decided to recover from our escapades in Amsterdam. Jackson and I were reassured by the different stages we saw erected throughout the city.

I specifically planned this part of the trip because my birthday was right in the middle of the music festival. I had great anticipation for this celebration. Music always put me in a good mood, and I couldn't think of a more memorable way to spend my birthday in the middle of a world famous music festival. The next day was going to be epic, and I would turn nineteen (or so I thought).

———————————

I was fired up when I woke up that morning. I was whistling full blast in the shower. The music was starting at noon, and it was time to celebrate.

There were several stages in the same park where we had seen the Reformation Wall, and there were plenty of places to get refreshments. Jackson said he would buy my drinks all day. We found one stage with a cool-looking band and grabbed drinks immediately.

Jackson bought two sangrias and two glasses of red wine as the band was warming up. There had to be twenty instruments on stage. A bald lanky man with sunglasses walked up to the microphone and paused for a minute. He tapped the mike a couple of times, and then he spoke.

"Tasty . . . Tasty . . . Strawberries . . . Tasty."

I looked at Jackson, and he looked back. We were just going with the groove, and it sounded cool to us. Then, that band got going, and they were serious. It was like an upbeat jazz ensemble with trumpets and bongos. It was really great music. Jackson and I listened to that whole concert and made our way to other bands in the vicinity. I had some kind of guide with me explaining the festival bands, but it was kind of confusing. We just went to whatever sounded best.

After spending the day listening to music, the rock came out that night. There was this Jewish band just tearing it up. It was almost heavy metal. We had consumed many drinks by then. The music got heavier and heavier, and Jackson and I ended up in a mosh pit. We banged against strangers with no regard. It was the first time I had ever done that. I couldn't feel anything anyways, so it was pretty fun.

The music died down, but there were lots of people sitting in a large grassy area. I still had that little bit of weed with me and rolled a joint. I think I dropped like half of it but managed to create something worthwhile. I sat next to some strangers, made crazy conversation, and lit it up.

After some time passed, we heard this banging coming from behind us. A drum line had formed out of nowhere. There were about ten people carrying anything that made a sound, and they put together this crazy beat. It was a rush, and Jackson and I danced late into the night until they stopped.

Around sunrise, Jackson and I staggered up the hilly city back to the hostel, which was much more family oriented. We tried to be quiet, but laughter set in. Jackson was on the top bunk; I was on the bottom. I let out a short burst of giggling, and he returned the act. It was like Club Van der Dookie or the pizza incident all over again, but there was really no reason to be laughing. It lasted a good while, and somehow we fell asleep.

About five hours later, I woke up Jackson, who was struggling a little bit.

I proclaimed, "That was one of the coolest birthdays ever. Thanks, man."

"Yeah, that was wild. What time is it?" Jackson asked.

"It's like ten, I think. I'll check."

In my attempt to gather the time, I found out some shocking news. I looked down at someone's watch, and it read 10:30. The shocking part was that it also read June 16, my real birthday. I had celebrated for a whole day, fully convinced it was my birthday, on the wrong day. I busted out laughing at my stupidity.

In the original plans, I was going to celebrate my nineteenth birthday in Geneva during the music festival. Since we didn't go back to Munich for a day, I lost a day somewhere during our travels. Oh yeah, being stoned out of our minds for four days didn't help either.

Well, today was my real birthday, so I decided to celebrate it again. I knew for sure it was the right date, and it just made it that much better. I thought about all my birthdays up to this point. I reminisced about my sixteenth birthday in Spain.

Señor Jose Garcia was one of the coolest teachers I've ever had. We just called him Mr. G. At my high school, he was the second-year Spanish teacher. I was a sophomore, and I began his class without much anticipation. I already knew him because his younger brother, Gabriel, was our age. Gabriel was an excellent soccer player, one of the best in the area. His other brother had played at the Catholic high school, and he went on to play college ball at Furman. Their father was a pediatrician with a great personality. Overall, the Garcias were a wonderful family.

Mr. G. was about twenty-five when he taught our class. He seemed older than that to us. Let's just say he wasn't in very good shape. But he was a jolly fellow who encouraged rebellion. He had an interesting past that led him up to teaching us. Mr. G. was a sucker for music, especially Phish, to the extreme, actually.

Mr. G. never owned a car until he was twenty-two. In fact, he never even had a license. He rationalized that it wasn't necessary unless you were going to drive.

During his college days, he decided to pick up and follow Phish. He did it for over a year. We didn't hear a lot about his experiences during this time other than he had grown dreadlocks. We weren't quite old enough to understand the lifestyle of following a band. I do remember him saying he had met the band in Europe. He was a groupie to the max. To be honest, he was probably living like those hippies I despised at Bonaroo. I wasn't old enough to understand, and he was a cool teacher, so I liked him.

While teaching our class, he would take off on the weekends to see a Phish show, no matter where it was. One time, he drove up to New York for a show. It was always funny when he returned. His nose would be glowing red, his eyes bloodshot, and his throat aching. The Mondays after a musical weekend were not the pinnacle of learning. Mr. G. told us he just needed some of Grandpa's Cough Syrup. It was a homemade mixture of hot tea, honey, and bourbon. He claimed it cured any kind of cold. It knocked him out enough to recover as well.

Mr. G. had a rebellious mentality. In his own way, he challenged the lifestyle of the kids from our privileged neighborhood. You wouldn't find Mr. G. sipping a scotch on the rocks at the country club after a round of golf with the fellows. He just thought differently, and it made the class interesting.

One time I commented on another teacher's religion. Our previous Spanish teacher had created a progressive church downtown, and it differed from the fundamentals of the Catholic church. I felt comfortable with Mr. G. so I asked him if our previous teacher was in a cult.

Mr. G. leaned back in his chair and said in a challenging way, "Isn't all religion a cult?"

Let's just say Mr. G. wasn't a fan of the establishment. Well, he was a fan of the Castilian form of Spanish, which originated near Madrid. Mr. G. believed the international presence of the Spanish language was good, but he also felt that most of the world butchered the language. In an attempt for his students to embrace the real Spanish, he organized a summer trip to Salamanca, Spain, an hour northeast of Madrid.

Salamanca was the home of the University of Salamanca, the oldest university in Spain. Mr. G. had been there several times, and he contacted a school named Collegio Delibes. The school invited international students, and the administrators helped arrange accommodations with hosting families.

When he offered the trip, I hopped on it in a heartbeat. After everything was said and done, seventeen of us signed up to go. There were fourteen guys and three girls.

There was just one little clause in the contract of travel that made the trip way over the top. Spain has no drinking age. Mr. G. knew that, and he wrote a permission form for the parents to sign that would allow us to have a glass of wine at dinner. This eliminated liability for him if anything went wrong. Let's just say we took advantage of that clause.

We left in early June, and the group would study at Collegio Delibes for a month. The flight was long, and we took the hour-long bus ride to the middle of Salamanca. There was a group of older Spanish women waiting for us when we arrived. The seventeen of us made our way off of the bus, gathered our luggage, and split into groups with our assigned family.

My roommate for the trip was Thomas James (TJ) Horton. We went to different middle schools, but we had become close through Buddy. I actually became really close to their family, and his mom referred to me as her other child. I had a habit of gravitating toward big families throughout my childhood. It gave me a sense of inclusion while also granting me the needed solitude for being an only child. In retrospect, I was always looking for a father figure to fill the void. Some families provided this in some way, but it was not their responsibility to teach me how to grow up. I now recognize that my one parent family was the hand I was dealt, and all I could do was my best given the situation. Regardless of why I got so attached to the Hortons, they were a caring family, and TJ was a close friend.

Our Spanish madre took us to her apartment building. She unlocked the bottom floor door, and we followed her up two flights of stairs. She opened the apartment to the right, and it was empty. It was a full apartment with three bedrooms, a living area, a balcony, and a kitchen. It turns out that the family lived across the hallway in a completely separate apartment. For the most part, we had the place to ourselves. At least, there was no direct supervision.

TJ and I shared a bedroom with two beds. We did have roommates in the other rooms. One guy was about twenty-one with glasses and a ponytail. He was from Poland and going to school to become a Spanish teacher. Another one of our roommates was on the French national hockey team. Then, there was Simone from Switzerland, who knew six different languages. Our Spanish family was running a camp for exchange students. Monetarily, I'm sure it made sense as well.

We got settled in and went straight to bed to ease the jet lag. There would be a lot of sleeping on this trip. The siesta is a wonderful thing.

The next day, we gathered as a class at the school. It was about a two-mile walk, and the trip provided excellent exercise throughout the trip. If we wanted to go anywhere, we had to walk. As indulgent as I was during that month, I ended up losing ten pounds.

Mr. G. sat us down and explained the rules of conduct. TJ and I realized quickly that we had a party pad, and we informed the "cool" kids that this was to be the gathering spot. Mr. G. warned that if we broke the rules, we would be sent home. He tried to be serious, but it was hard to grasp. After the meeting, we were free to explore the city.

Buddy and I had plans of our own. We went to a grocery store and bought a large bottle of the beer Mahou Cinco Estrella. Well, Buddy and I sat on a bench close to the town square and consumed our beverage that afternoon. Man, did we get some dirty looks from the locals as they strolled by. Just because there was no drinking age does not mean that everybody and their brother drinks all day. During the trip, I found out that not having a drinking age actually helped people have a better grasp on using alcohol.

Now, in America, you cannot drink until you are twenty-one. I think this totally screws people up. I am in total agreement with the sentiment that if you can take a bullet for your country, you should be able to enjoy a beer. On the other hand, people rely on transportation by car much more in the States. Although I did it many times, drinking and driving is one of the stupidest things you can do.

Back to the concept of age and consumption. I saw it growing up, and I really thought the way we drank was normal. People, at least the people I knew, drank to get as fucked up as possible. I never considered having just one glass of wine with a good meal or having just a couple of beers during a football game. It was always balls to the wall.

College didn't help much either. Thousands of students have died from alcohol poisoning. It really is a tragedy, but it is related to the culture surrounding the beverage. Because it's not legal to drink, people consume immense amounts in a short amount of time, thinking this is the way to loosen up. This approach is intriguing, and doing something illegal makes it that much more fun.

Fraternity and sorority life thrives on alcohol. Most of them probably couldn't function without it. I remember one UNC football game; we went early to pregame, and at nine o'clock in the morning, people were funneling beers. Before taking it down, the developing alcoholic would scream "Frat!" just to make fun of the concept. It was actually kind of funny at the time.

Spain thinks a little different. I'm not saying people don't get drunk, but how many rehab centers do you think there are in Europe? Teens were allowed to drink at dinner under their parents' supervision. This eliminated sneaking around to get drunk. There was guidance in the way to drink. It made much more sense to me. Did I fully embrace it? Well, of course not. But it made me feel better to understand the different cultures.

The seventeen of us would attend class from eight to two during the weekdays. That was it. We were free to do whatever we wanted after that. TJ and I would walk back to our residence, and our madre would feed us a big meal during the two-hour siesta. During this time, the whole city would shut down. Sometimes we would fall asleep after eating and not wake up until around nine o'clock, when we would eat dinner. The lifestyle was awesome and very stress free.

School was boring at times, and we actually learned more just being in the environment. Ordering a meal at a restaurant taught us more about Spanish than learning grammar. The seventeen of us were divided into sections by how well we knew the language. There was elementary, intermediate, and advanced. My other good friend, Harry, was in the elementary section.

Now some of the teachers we had were hot Spanish women. During one class, Harry had to speak in front of the class, and he was trying to ask how to say the word for ice cream. In his attempt, he pretended to hold an imaginary cone and lick it. Unfortunately, it looked like he was giving a blowjob. The teacher thought he was a pervert, and the whole class laughed at him. What a goof.

Harry also liked to talk a lot of shit when he got drunk. Many times, we came very close to having violent altercations with Spanish natives. Harry knew very little Spanish at the time. When you are talking shit to someone who speaks another language, they obviously can't grasp the content of your putdowns.

In his attempt to translate a rude remark, Harry yelled at a group of guys, "Put your boca on my piña." He was trying to say "put your mouth on my dick," but what he really shouted was "put your mouth on my pineapple." Needless to say, the Spanish guys looked extremely perplexed. How are you going to fight somebody when they're talking about pineapples? There will be more to come about Harry down the road.

Salamanca had a vibrant nightlife, and my friends and I took full advantage of the drinking clause. A group of us would gather at my party pad and drink beer until we were ready to go out. Salamanca actually had a bar where all they served were shots. This was like heaven for fifteen—and sixteen-year-olds.

So my birthday fell right in the middle of this month-long trip abroad. I was turning sixteen, a special birthday. I would soon be driving that 4Runner I had saved up for since I was in eighth grade.

Mr. G. had been doing his own thing during the trip. Yes, he was our supervisor, and he did give us some guidance. However, he had his own apartment, and he pretty much laid the ground rules at the beginning and let us roam. When our parents found out about this strategy later, they were irate. By that time, the trip was over, and nobody had been seriously hurt, so what could they do? Out of all the stories, Harry and TJ gave them the most concern, and it happened to occur on my birthday.

Mr. G. knew it was my birthday so he invited me to have a beer. I asked TJ, Harry, and Buddy to come along. We went into a bar and sat down. We felt so mature. Mr. G. bought me a Delirium Tremens, a Belgian beer with about 10 percent alcohol. My tolerance wasn't that high as a newly dawned sixteen-year-old, so I was drunk after two of them. Everybody else that was there had two as well. We were all pretty buzzed and having a grand ol' time. There was a rerun of a US soccer game playing, and we personified the stereotypical obnoxious American, yelling every time the ball went in the air. Spaniards don't like Americans too much; they just called us gringos.

My birthday pals left the bar a little tipsy to say the least. Mr. G. knew his limitations, so he planned to walk us back to the town square and head his own way. On the way back, the shit hit the fan. Mr. G., Buddy, and I walked in front while Harry and TJ were joking around behind us.

TJ and Harry got a little aggressive like some guys do, and it just took an absolute turn for the worse. Harry put TJ in a headlock. TJ got upset and punched Harry in the balls. Then, Harry let loose. You just don't punch a guy in the balls. It's right up there with the Golden Rule.

Harry stood TJ up, grabbed him by the shoulders, and head-butted the shit out of him. It was like a Kung Fu movie. TJ took the full brunt of force and flew back into a window and slumped down. His nose was on the side of his face, and blood was gushing out of it.

Mr. G. freaked out and yelled at Buddy to go home. He scampered off like there was no tomorrow. I ran to assist, but TJ's nose was bleeding like a freaking waterfall. TJ needed to go to the hospital and fast. Harry grabbed his nuts in pain and repeatedly apologized to the dazed TJ.

Thank God Mr. G. was there. We got to a cab stop, and he had to beg to get a ride. Some drivers flat out refused, fearing TJ would get blood all over the backseat. We finally got a Good Samaritan driver, and we all piled in to the cab and headed for the hospital.

All we had to do now is rely on Socialist medicine. What a joke. The cab pulled up to the emergency room, Mr. G. took TJ inside, and Harry and I waited outside. Harry was sure he would be sent home, but I tried to convince him otherwise. We ended up waiting until four in the morning, so we covered a variety of topics of conversation to bide the time.

TJ and Mr. G. emerged from the sliding doors; the doctor had concluded that his nose was not broken. That was simply astonishing. Luckily, TJ wears glasses, and he has been able to cover up the battle wound ever since. But if he takes those suckers off, his nose is crooked as the Mafia. In a nutshell, that was my sixteenth birthday. Now, I was in Geneva about to celebrate my nineteenth birthday for the second time.

11

Once again, Jackson and I started drinking early. We made our way to the different stages and really tried to embrace the variety of music that was offered. We listened to a choir. We listened to an orchestra. We listened to a solo violinist. Then we went and bought a bottle of Johnny Walker. I'm sorry, but we didn't have a tremendous attention span, and our mission was pretty direct: party, party, party. The day turned to evening, and half the bottle of Johnny Walker was gone. Somehow, we made it up to the top of the Reformation Wall. There was a band set up to begin around ten o'clock. It was a Doors cover band. Perfect.

The cover band played all the favorites: "LA Woman," "Light My Fire," "Gloria," "People Are Strange," and "Riders on the Storm." The list goes on. Those guys on stage rocked it hard for over two hours. During that time, we staggered and sputtered the words. There were some American girls near us, and we kept antagonizing them to take pulls from our bottle of scotch. They looked at us like we were crazy, which we were in a way.

The band ended, and Jackson and I made our way back down to the park below. There was still a large gathering of people. No drum line this time, but we met three cute girls. I thought I might be getting an extra special birthday present.

I had the very last of the weed, and we all sat in a circle and shared it. One of the girls was from Chile, and that's all I really remember. After some conversation and flirting, they invited us back to their apartment. We stopped at a store on the way and picked up a bottle of rum. Bad, bad idea. At least for me.

That scotch already had my number. While I thought I was teasing our new female friends, I was actually being pretty confrontational. Jackson attested to this the next day, since I soon blacked out. I do remember entering their apartment and sitting at the kitchen table. I poured myself a big glass of rum, took a couple of gulps, and passed out face first on the table. My birthday had ended right then and there.

Jackson had much more composure on this night, and he was going for the kill with the Chilean. He woke me up and put me in a cab back to the hostel. I found myself back in the hostel bed the next morning, so I obviously made it somehow.

Well, that bastard Jackson was getting all the action. He went back into the bedroom with the South American, and they caressed and kissed. He then made his way back to the kitchen and just whipped it out. He lay down, and she slobbed his nob on the kitchen floor while the sun came up. He was living the adolescent dream. I was down for the count.

The final day of the festival had arrived. Jackson and I had a blast so far, and we felt sad that the music was coming to an end. We had already made arrangements to take a late train over the Alps and back to Munich. We had a good amount of the day to soak in the scenery.

Before starting our exploration around Lake Geneva, we stopped in a small bar to have a beer. It was right around lunchtime. We had gone to another Italian restaurant on this street the day before to watch one of the soccer matches, so it seemed plausible that there would be other places to eat. It was kind of a back street off of the main road in an okay part of town.

When we walked into the bar, it was mighty dark, and the décor was filled with red velvet. There was also an entry in the back covered by two black curtains. Jackson and I just wanted a beer, so we sat down. Not too much talking took place, just grunts related to the night before.

A lady in her midforties, maybe older, sat at the end of the bar. She had a long cigarette holder, and she puffed small clouds of smoke as Jackson and I drank our beers. I noticed her when I turned that way, but it was nothing special. She was talking with another man who looked like a regular.

The dark-haired woman was wearing a sleek, all-black garment with touches of lace in spots a fortysomething-year-old shouldn't be wearing. After several minutes, she made her way over to where Jackson and I were sitting.

As she approached, she put her hands on our shoulders like we were old friends. Let's call her Esmeralda.

"You two men look like young strong American boys. Correct?"

"Yes, we are. Can we help you?" I replied.

I was already annoyed, but she continued the conversation. "You are staying in Geneva, yes? It is a wonderful city. A place of much culture."

"Agree. It's a nice place."

"How about you buy a woman a drink?"

"Look, I don't think so, lady. We won't be here that long."

"Oh come on, baby. You know it will be worth it. There is even a special place we can go and share it."

I looked over at Jackson, who had an insulting smirk on his face. I knew he was making fun of me without saying a word. He also had it pretty good last night, so he had nothing to complain about. There was nothing like insulting at an old friend.

Anyways, Esmeralda was laying it on thick. Let's just say she had plenty of resources to complete this task. Stairmaster, pilates, and thighmaster were probably not in her vocabulary.

Esmeralda took her finger and ran it down her blouse while saying, "Are you scared of what I have to offer?"

"Damn it, woman," I barked. "I am not scared of what you have to offer. I don't even know what you are talking about. Leave me alone!"

"Fine. I will be waiting over there when you are ready."

"Cool. Good talk."

Jackson punched me in the arm when she left, saying, "Man, you should go tag that."

"Yeah, you're right, cougar-slayer. Just another one to check off the list, you ass. I mean, what the hell was that about?"

"I think she likes you, dude. You got to slay the dragons before you get to the princess. Go for it."

"Man, I have a strange feeling about this place. We need to get out of here. Finish your beer and let's go."

As we took our last sips, we saw another semi-elderly woman "escorting" a man to the back. Yeah, I figured out what was going on. We were in another fucking whorehouse. I mean, what the hell? We couldn't seem to get away from these damn things. I must just be a walking boner looking for a place to crash for a bit. It's not like I meant to go in that place, it just happened. Son of a bitch.

Jackson didn't quite catch on so I let him make fun of me a little longer. As we exited, he threw another verbal jab.

"Man, you just get all the hotties, don't you, big guy?" Jackson thought he was being real sly. "I mean, she was totally all over your nuts."

This is when I started to mess with him a little.

"Dude, you think I could have gotten some afternoon delight? You know, lay the pipe like a real man. Bang a rang like it ain't no thang."

I had a big smile on my face the whole time.

"Yes! You had it in there, dude. I mean she was butt ugly, but why not?"

"Maybe because she was a fucking prostitute, you idiot."

"What? For real?"

"Yes, you retard. Didn't you see the back room?"

"No man, I just thought she was horny."

I couldn't help but laugh. I put my arm around Jackson's shoulder for a minute as we walked down the street.

"I love you, man, but I think you only have half a brain."

"I got a fully functioning penis to make up for it."

"Touche. Now, let's go hop in the lake. It's getting hot as hell. I'm sure your penis will guide the way toward some decent-looking girls."

Even though we were practically in the Alps, Geneva was quite warm that day. The lake looked more appealing after every minute that passed. The city was at the tip of the lake, and parts of it extended around each side. We decided to go down one side and find a place to swim and cool off.

Jackson and I walked for about half a mile and came across a stone ramp. We agreed that this would do. It didn't really matter where we got in; we just wanted to get into the water. Unfortunately, we picked a bad entry point.

Jackson took off his shirt and shoes and ran down the stone ramp toward the water. The ramp had algae all over it, and it was slick as glass. He busted his ass like a true klutz.

I, of course, burst out in laughter as he lay in pain. Jackson pulled himself up and finally made it into the water. He was bruised, but I could tell the water was worth it. Then I made my attempt to get in.

Seeing how Jackson had just hurt himself, I walked carefully down the ramp, yelling out at Jackson about how stupid he was. Then, it happened. I hit a slick spot and busted my ass even worse than Jackson did. My feet came right out from underneath me, and I made solid contact with the wet stones. Brilliant move, Cam, brilliant move.

Now it was Jackson's turn to talk some shit. After several minutes of banter, we agreed on a truce because we had both obviously suffered injuries on the way into the clear blue water. Then, we just floated around. The water was cold, but it felt awesome. The lake was so clean. All of the drinking we had been doing the night before seemed to dissipate from our bodies. That lake was extremely refreshing. We must have spent thirty minutes just floating and swimming back and forth. However, there was still the problem of going back up the slippery ramp to get out of the water.

"All right, I'll go first," I proclaimed.

"Good luck. Show me the way, and I'll be right behind you.

Thinking I would have more grace on the way up than the way down, I stood upright and started to climb out of the water. Of course, it didn't work. I slipped again and managed to brace myself with my outstretched arms. I started crawling out but kept slipping back down. After multiple attempts to claw my way up, I grasped solid enough ground to get off the wretched ramp. Jackson followed suit, and after a good amount of effort, he made it out too.

We walked away from the city and found a landmark confirming our lack of patience and immense lack of common sense. As we turned a corner, we saw a large beach right there in front of us. There were a ton of people soaking in the sun. On the other hand, Jackson and I were beginning to dry off under the sun with our newly acquired cuts and bruises on full display.

We walked along the beach. There were girls all around. I thought about making up for the ugly prostitute in the whorehouse, but we had to return to the hostel, gather our bags, and get on a train in the next two hours, so a pickup attempt didn't seem worth it. We weren't really going to accomplish anything in the time we had. It was possible to meet a complete stranger, hook up real quick, and leave town, but not very likely. I just had to cut my losses.

We made it onto the train and embarked on another lengthy trip. Geneva wasn't exactly close to Munich. We had to travel though the Alps, and it would take about eight hours, not really something we were looking forward to.

Time went by in intervals. Sometimes thirty minutes would fly by. Other times, five minutes would seem like an hour. Looking out into the mountains from the train was interesting, but it lost its luster pretty quickly. Luckily, there was a restaurant car in the middle where we could grab some dinner. Jackson and I went there about halfway through the ride.

As it was getting dark outside, we sat down at a table. There was nothing better to do, so a lengthy meal would make the trip go by faster. Once again, we tried to process all the events that had transpired so far. The World Cup journey was halfway over, and we already had enough stories for a lifetime.

Jackson and I didn't see too much of each other during my freshman year of college. We stayed in touch, knowing that we would embark on this trip for the summer. Given our few conversations during my freshman year, this was a good time to catch up on our first year out of high school.

Surprisingly, we had not gotten sick of each other yet. I guess we were having too much fun for either one of us to get sensitive. Our spirits were high, and there was excitement around each turn.

We looked forward to spending more time in Munich. We had only been there for a couple of nights when we arrived, and then we took off through three other countries. The upcoming week in Munich would give a chance to really soak in the city. We hadn't even been to a beer garden, something Germany was famous for.

Since we had had such time apart from each other during that first year of college, it was fun to share some stories. Most of Jackson's consisted of trips to Athens and football games. That place is a haven for attractive girls and partying. He was only able to make it a couple of times, but those times were like heaven compared to the military life he was living in north Georgia.

Jackson managed to have sex with a girl on the roof of a fraternity house during a football game in August. He had burn marks on his knees from the hot shingles. Apparently, the girl's dad was there and tried to fight Jackson in the front yard; seems she was still in high school. Imagine how Daddy felt about his sweet little girl after that one.

Overall, it was a good decision for Jackson to start out in military school. He transferred after his second year, but it formulated some kind of foundation that kept him at bay. Sort of.

We remained in the dining car for quite a long time. Jackson was interested in my experiences at Chapel Hill. Going two states away for college was a big step for someone from Ellington. At least I felt that way. Most people went to Georgia or Georgia Tech. There were exceptions, but this was mostly the case. Despite the poor high school educational system in Georgia, my class had some extremely intelligent students. When it came down to crunch time for deciding where to go to college, I thought everybody would really step outside of the box. My peers were more than qualified to go to schools all over the country. But most ended up going to UGA. I was bitter about this for some reason. It was not my place to tell people where to go; but by that time, I was ready to leave Ellington and get away from the place I had spent all of my life.

I now realize that it was fine for those people to go to UGA. It was a big school, and they were able to find their independence if that's what they wanted. Even sticking with a group of people they felt comfortable with from home didn't mean they wouldn't ever venture outside of the familiar. It just maybe wasn't their time.

Early on, I did make an effort to stay in touch with my friends from Ellington. I probably tried a little too hard. As Jackson and I sat on the train, I recounted a trip I had made to Sewanee a couple months before to see TJ.

Sewanee is a small private school very close to where we went to Bonaroo. The school had an annual Spring Party Weekend, which was supposed to be pretty wild. I rarely turned down the opportunity to be a part of something like that. TJ encouraged me to visit for their biggest weekend of the year.

Chapel Hill to Sewanee. That's the middle of North Carolina to the southwestern part of Tennessee. Andy, a friend from school, was from Raleigh, and he had a friend at Sewanee that he wanted to visit for Spring Party Weekend as well. Andy's girlfriend went to the University of South Carolina, and he and I made several trips during the fall to attend football games. I was sure this would be another great road trip.

It takes about eight hours to get from Chapel Hill to Sewanee, and I had a plan on how to make a little extra cash out of the trip. I had been behaving more and more unruly, and I made some moves and ended up buying an ounce of weed. I figured I could come out on top by about a hundred and fifty bucks by flipping it over the weekend. I hadn't dealt drugs much, but it seemed like a good idea at the time. I made the purchase earlier in the week, and I was ready to leave that Thursday. One problem: Andy bailed at the last minute.

I haven't mentioned this yet, but from time to time my temper would flare up. Andy's late notice got me pretty pissed, and I decided to just make the trip on my own. I just said, "Fuck it," and took off in my car.

To prepare for the trip, I took part of my stash and rolled two big joints for the road. It was going to be a long trip, so I needed something to keep me occupied.

It was a pretty straight shot all the way on I-40. The interstate winds through Greensboro, Winston-Salem, Asheville, Knoxville, and Chattanooga. The Appalachian Mountains happen to be in the way, so the interstate kind of makes an S to get over. Once I got close to Greensboro, I lit up one of my left-handed cigarettes.

At some point near Asheville, I made a pit stop. After leaving the gas station, I got back on I-40 going east, the wrong direction. You think I would have figured that out, but I was a complete dumbass. I was in Asheville and drove almost all the way back to Greensboro. That was two hours of driving in the wrong direction.

I kept seeing familiar signs of places I had already passed. Were there really two Winston-Salems in North Carolina? Well, I finally realized my mistake and turned around. This blunder added an extra four hours to my trip. I was pissed, but what could I really do about it? I was determined to make it, so I kept on keeping on.

It was late when I approached Knoxville. I had already smoked the other joint, and it was beginning to rain pretty hard. There is a stretch of highway on I-40 that isn't the most comforting in the world. The slope is extremely steep, and eighteen-wheelers have to drive in the right lane. There are huge dirt ramps to the side that are supposed to protect the trucks if their brakes go out. I guess they are just supposed to slow down going up the slope. It was kind of amateurish.

There was a lot of construction as I drove through Knoxville. So here I was, driving my small Honda Accord in the pouring rain, through construction, next to eighteen-wheelers, on the steepest part of I-40, after eight hour of being behind the wheel. Oh yeah, my brain was covered in THC, making me even more paranoid of the adverse travel conditions. There was just no way I was going to make it without pulling over for the night.

As much as I wanted to gut it out, I decided to pull into a motel around twelve o'clock. Throughout the trip, TJ had been calling me to check on my status. I kept telling him that I was running a little behind schedule. He was a worrier, but I didn't pay much attention. When I let him know I was pulling over, he figured something out of the ordinary had happened.

In my mind, it was just a little bump in the road. So I slept in this grungy motel and woke up the next morning and got back on the road. After grinding it out, I pulled up to the Sewanee's isolated campus.

Well, damn it if I didn't know that this place was pretty much the polar opposite of Chapel Hill. At Sewanee, they don't have cell phones. Everybody used a freaking dorm phone. There just wasn't any service. Somehow, the students took solace in this and tried to turn it into a cool thing. In the scheme of things, it was really just a pain in the ass. There were some other things that made this place very foreign to me.

The dorms had moms. Yes, elderly women who lived in the dorms with the students. They were caretakers who provided comfort and guidance. I really didn't get this either. Why would you want an old lady to be around you in college? It worked for them, but it did not seem very liberating.

Before the trip, I asked TJ what kind of liquor he wanted me to bring. He said he wanted a handle of Maker's Mark, so I dropped the cash and picked one up in Chapel Hill. We were old friends, and a nice bottle of liquor would be a good gesture.

The Greek life in Sewanee picked up in the spring instead of the fall. I think this is actually a better way of doing things. Freshmen get an idea of what each fraternity and sorority are like before they take the plunge. Unfortunately, TJ was in the last stretch of pledging, which created some problems. His duty for that Friday night was to stay up all night and cook a pig.

The main attraction of Spring Party Weekend is that the school hosts a band. The inclement weather I ran into going through Knoxville had not let up. Usually, the band performs outside, but the weather was just too bad. They had to move it inside the school auditorium, even though it wasn't very big.

TJ was running around taking orders from older brothers, so it was really hard for me to get in touch with him. Another friend from Ellington, John Glenn, had made the trip from Columbia, South Carolina with some of his friends. He was a longtime buddy who grew up right down the street from me. We were distantly related through Ellington's Irish Catholic Mafia. Whenever I went down to USC with Andy, I stayed with John.

The band for the weekend was Bone Thugz and Harmony. Interesting choice for a small preppy private school, but everyone was excited. Everybody wanted a piece of the action. John and I started drinking bourbon in some girl's room near the auditorium.

We decided to play a practical joke on this kid we'll call Jim before the band performed. John had migraines from time to time, and to remedy the problem, he always carried some BC Headache Powder. Like it sounds, it's a pouch of powder you either put in water or straight on the tongue.

Jim was in the same room as we got ready for the concert. John let me know he had the headache powder, and we knew the kid was pretty impressionable. We had a joke in mind, and it played out well. John and I had to take a leak, and we went to the hallway bathroom to relieve ourselves. Jim popped in the door soon after.

By that time, John had pulled out his pouch of BC Headache Powder. John was not afraid to put on a serious face for a rewarding laugh. He enticed Jim by asking him a question.

"Hey, man. You want to do some cocaine?"

"I don't know, man. I've never done it before."

"Come on. It's Spring Party Weekend. This is some good shit right here."

"I mean, I guess I can be convinced to do anything."

It was a strange statement from Jim, but he obviously had low self-esteem. We didn't care about that at all.

"All right, Jim. Come in the stall and we'll cut a line out for you. It's going to be awesome. Completely awesome."

The three of us squeezed into a stall to complete the prank on this gullible kid. I pulled out a twenty and rolled it up. John made a line of powder with his credit card on the top of the tank.

"All right, go ahead. Let her rip," John encouraged.

"You sure this stuff is straight?" Jim asked.

"For sure. Now are you going to do it or not?"

"Yeah, yeah, I will."

Jim put the rolled-up bill to his nose and ripped that thick line of white powder. That dummy did a line of BC Headache Powder off the toilet seat, thinking it was cocaine. John and I busted out laughing after the first sound of his snort.

"Dude, that's pretty good," Jim said, surprised.

In between spurts of laughter, John replied, "Yeah, dude. You killed it."

I chimed in so we could split, "All right, nice doing drugs with you. We got to go. Don't go dying on us now."

John and I burst out of the bathroom and ran back to our bourbon and Cokes. The concert had already started, and we had to get moving. We gulped down the rest of our drinks and headed out into the pouring rain.

When we got to the front of the building, it was a shitshow. There was a group of about fifty people shouting and screaming outside the building. The auditorium had reached full capacity, and no one else was allowed in; it would break the fire code. It was the most anticipated event of the year, and the outraged students were beginning to riot.

John and I didn't know any better, so we joined right in, cussing and screaming for justice. College kids could get pretty worked up, even about the stupidest things. Regardless, we were stuck out in the pouring rain, listening to the echoes of rap from inside.

This conundrum was not satisfactory. I had driven over eleven hours to get to this place, and I was not about to miss the concert. We snuck around to the side, and someone had already thrown a rock through one of the stained glass windows.

"Cam, we are going to hop through that window."

"All right. I'll give you a lift."

I hoisted John up into the window so he could crawl through. We could see flashes of lights from the security guards inside, so we waited for the right time to enter.

John was already in, and he pulled me up. I cut my knee on some broken glass and fell into the building. Immediately, security came after us. John ripped off his shirt and ran into the crowd. I took off the other way. Not according to plan, I ran away from the security and straight into a group of police officers standing backstage.

They saw that I was soaked, and the guy chasing me arrived and confirmed that I had broken into the auditorium. One of the cops took me aside and asked for my ID.

Not wanting to get in trouble for drinking under age, I handed him an old North Carolina driver's license a friend had given me in Chapel Hill. Sounds like a bad move, but I played it off fine.

This was the middle of nowhere in Tennessee, and I wasn't dealing with the brightest cat in the world. I convinced that cop that the license was mine. Big surprise, he was still being a dick.

"Son, where is your car?"

"Sir, it's somewhere on the other side of this campus. I have been drinking so I can't drive anywhere."

"I'm going to need you to leave the campus or you have to come with me."

"I'm not driving anywhere, sir."

"All right then."

He handcuffed me and put me in the back of his cop car. I was sitting behind a Plexiglas window in the backseat. The sirens went on, and he carried me off to the station. Well, it was more of a drunk tank for students on campus. We got inside his office, and he sat me down.

"Now son, who are you here with?" the cop inquired. "I can't let you go unless someone comes to pick you up."

"Thomas James Horton."

The officer picked up the phone and called TJ's dorm room. Luckily, TJ was there. Kind of. I could only hear the officer's voice as he held my fake ID in his hand.

"Yes, Thomas. This is Officer Jones. Do you know a Franklin Johnson from North Carolina?"

Officer Jones nodded his head, glared at me, and dropped the driver's license on the desk. TJ had told him he didn't know anybody by that name, which obviously was not helpful. I got a sinking feeling in my stomach.

"Let me see your real ID, son," the cop ordered.

I had no choice, and I reached into my wallet and gave him my Georgia ID. The cop wrote me up for criminal impersonation, a Class B misdemeanor. I was mortified. This was the first legal trouble I had ever been in. Criminal impersonation sounded horrible. How was I ever going to get a job with that on my record? I was pretty freaked out.

TJ rode his bike down to the drunk tank to pick me up. He was pissed. I can't really blame him, but I was equally as mad. Not intentionally, but he had just fucked me over. I had the perfect cover, and he blew it. TJ was scared, because Sewanee had a strict honor code, and breaking it could have meant expulsion. I was too self-absorbed to think about this right then. I still felt betrayed, and we were not close pals for the moment.

TJ refused to listen to my story, and we walked back to his dorm in silence. He put me in his dorm and told me not to leave.

Miraculously, John found me in the dorm. He had been looking all over campus for me. He asked me to come back out, but I decided that was enough action for one night.

I went to sleep and woke up the next morning to find the empty bottle of Maker's Mark. TJ drank it with his pledge brothers while they cooked the pig all night. What the hell was going on? This weekend had turned to hell.

With much effort, I shook most of it off, and TJ and I reconciled our differences. Sewanee was just so opposite of Chapel Hill that I couldn't adjust quickly enough.

Looking back, it probably wasn't the most appealing thing for him: his friend had taken two days to get there, brought an ounce of weed with him, and then lied to a police officer, putting him in jeopardy. Despite all of the negatives, I managed to have a good time the next day and night, and I drove back to Chapel Hill in record time on Sunday.

In the end, it was a good story to share. My charges got dropped, and TJ and I actually laugh about it today. As for the middle of the train ride through the Alps, it made for good entertainment. The hours passed by more quickly as we shared more stories, and soon we were back to where we started: Munich.

12

That Monday was June 19. Jackson and I had left Ellington on June 6, and we were still full of energy. Now, it was time to conquer the beer gardens of Munich. Since we left Munich so soon after our arrival to Europe, there was now a solid week in which to explore the city. The first thing was to revisit Guido's. Jackson and I grabbed a pizza and really set our minds on exploring the historic city.

There was a large park in the middle of Munich named the English Garden. The weather was pleasant once again. We made our way to the park and wandered for a good amount of time. Soon, we stumbled across an area with tons of tables and lots of beer. We had found our first beer garden.

Beer gardens come in all different shapes and sizes. For the most part, it's a place that serves beer and has places to sit. It is not uncommon to order a beer and sit next to a complete stranger. Some places are more formal than others. The variations are tremendous, but the one we found in the park was quite popular.

There was a wooden structure where one lined up to get served. Jackson and I were thirsty, of course, and a nice beer would satisfy that in a heartbeat. I got up to the front to get a drink. One of the choices available was a mixture of beer and lemonade. I liked beer, and I liked lemonade. Maybe they would make a good combination. I took a sip after I picked it up, but it was not quite the best selection. It wasn't like it was going to be the only one. I could survive.

The amount of beer served is important to note as well. Most people know the stereotypical mug of Bavarian beer. The mugs they gave us were huge. Each stein had to hold at least forty ounces. Jackson ordered a different beer, and we grabbed an open bench. There was a big screen set up for one of the soccer matches, but it wasn't one of the more anticipated games. We didn't pay much attention. After downing our first round, we went back for more and returned to our seats. About halfway through the second round, a young lanky man with curly red hair and sunglasses asked if he could take a seat. We cordially granted him the honor of sitting with such esteemed individuals as ourselves.

"You lads enjoying the beer and football?" he asked with an Irish accent.

I piped right up. "Absolutely, we have been having a blast over here. You're from Ireland, right?"

"County Cork, born and raised. Go by the name of Paul."

"Cam."

"Jackson."

We all shook hands and had a friendly conversation. He told us of his travels across Europe and his time spent in Germany. As he spoke, I realized how many different kinds of people were in the beer garden. There were literally people from all over the world. All of us were mashed into one area enjoying a common drink of beer and watching the worldwide sport of soccer.

Jackson and I talked to Paul for several rounds of the large mugs of beer. I was getting drunk, and I reminisced over our travels away from Munich and our activities over the last week. He seemed like a cool guy, and I needed some advice about an upcoming event.

"So Paul, we went to Amsterdam for three days. You ever been there?"

"Oh sure, several times. Hard to pass up a weekend of legal drugs. Always stayed away from the prostitution though. Like to think I can get laid on my own. You have a good time there?"

"It was fun, but I couldn't live there. I got to ask you, though. We bought some mushrooms while we were there, and we need a good place to take them. You got any ideas?"

"Well, you know you need to be in nature, for one thing. Since you are in Munich, you can go to Wallberg Mountain. If you take the train south of here for about an hour and a half, you'll come to a town called Rottach-Egern. It is on Tegernsee Lake. There's a gondola that will take you to the top of the mountain. That should do you good."

"Paul, that sounds awesome."

It also sounded like something out of The Chronicles of Narnia, except for the gondola and the train, I guess. I was surprised at the recommendation, but there was no need to plan anything more than what Paul had suggested. That was an incredible idea.

"We'll do it tomorrow," I said. "You good with that, Jackson?"

"Hell, yeah."

Jackson and I thoroughly enjoyed the high spirits of our fellow traveler. We shared stories about our lives and kept good company until sunset. As the light faded, we bid farewell to our new friend. The beer garden was closing soon, and we went for our last round. We also grabbed a large turkey leg for dinner. It was time to get ready for another night out on the town. And this time, we had some absinthe.

Those heavy German beers did more damage than anticipated. When Jackson and I returned to the pad, we both passed out. I managed to set my alarm for nine o'clock just in case.

The alarm sounded, and when I woke up, I was still drunk. I was groggy, but I knew I couldn't pass up the night by sleeping. We were only in Germany once, remember? The bottle of absinthe was on the table in the middle of the room. The thought of drinking it propelled my body out of bed, and I woke Jackson. That's a good sign for a healthy relationship with alcohol, right?

I jumped on my pal and yelled, "Jackson! The room is on fire. Get up! Get up!"

"What the hell? All right, dude, let's go."

Jackson sprang out of bed and ran toward the door. When he reached the knob, he stopped.

"Wait. Fuck you, Cam. You're such an asshole!"

"Gotcha, bitch! Anyway, there is a bottle of absinthe on the table that needs some drinking."

"I'm taking a shower first. Got to wash off some of the ashes, you dick."

While I waited, I put on some tunes. Gator had a liking for the Grateful Dead. I spent plenty of time listening to music with him and got hooked on the Dead. As I played "Scarlet Begonias"/"Fire on the Mountain," I opened the door to the small balcony. There were some leftover cigarettes from one of our late nights, and I lit one up in the cool air. There seemed to be a progression of smoking the longer I stayed in Europe.

As I was jamming out to the heady tunes, Jackson yelled from inside, "All right, bitch. Let's get drunk!"

That's what I was looking for. I flicked the cigarette off the railing and stepped back inside. I grabbed the bottle of absinthe and held it in the air.

I looked at Jackson and said, "It's time, my friend. Grab some glasses."

Jackson was in and out of the kitchen in a flash. He never got a chance to drink the absinthe in Amsterdam, and he was eager to try it. I poured a large shot into each glass. I made a toast to Europe, and we gulped our drinks down.

In order to relish the bright green drink, we alternated with shots of vodka. Jackson and I decided we would go back to Kultfabrik. For the next hour, we alternated between the clear and green bottles. It didn't take long before we were heavily socially lubricated.

In no time, we made it back to the locale of our first night out. We went into one of the many bars in the area. The techno music was loud, and the overlapping beats seemed to be a little more profound than usual.

Jackson and I barged into the bar. I yelled for us to take some shots. Jackson put an order in for flaming shots. The bartender mixed the shots and lit them on fire, putting a straw in them before serving them to us. When she served mine, I lifted it to take it while it was still on fire. Jackson stopped me before I dumped the flaming liquid into my mouth. I just laughed, blew it out, and drank it down. We migrated away from the bar with a beer in hand. Not long after finishing it, I told Jackson to go get us some drinks. He came back with a bottle of vodka.

"Jackson, are you serious? I asked for a drink."

"This how my niggas do it!"

I figured, what the hell? My attitude changed quickly, and I gave in to the overindulgence. The last thing I remember was getting up on a high table. It had a round top just wide enough to stand on. As the alcohol coursed through my body and the music beats got faster, I tipped the table back and forth with my feet like a skateboard and yelled at the top of my lungs. Just a pure shout of energy. I could have been mistaken for a madman.

This drunkenness was a bit different than normal. Usually, the more I drank, the more my motor skills diminished, my speech slurred, and my coordination decreased. But this night, I felt in the zone. Not to say I wasn't wasted, but I felt like a focused and vigilant partier. Maybe absinthe was stronger than I thought.

We partied the night away. There may have been girls there. I don't really know. I just know I was having the best time since I stepped off the plane two weeks earlier.

On the way back to the subway, we decided to tempt fate. We couldn't believe our outlandish ways would have any repercussions. In the subway, certain areas were closed with metal gates. In my euphoria, I decided to pull off my shirt and place the collar on the top of my head like a turban. I ran up to the gates and shook them violently. Jackson and I were in somewhat of a maze, so we just kept running around aimlessly, screaming at the top of our lungs.

We ran around the corner, and two policemen were waiting for us. They motioned for us to come to them, and in the process, I slid my shirt back on inside out.

"What are you doing?" one of the officers said.

Without hesitation, I said, "Officer, we are lost." While still trying to adjust my shirt, I continued, "We are sorry. Please don't arrest us."

In an American situation, we would have been cuffed fairly quickly, maybe beaten with a billy club for disturbing the peace, and possibly degraded by some cop on an ego trip. These cops were completely different.

One of the policemen put his finger up to his mouth and said, "Be quiet and go home."

Jackson and I didn't blink an eye. We turned around and walked slowly toward the subway. We both believed we were going to jail just minutes earlier. Once the train pulled up, we cheered that we had defied the law of the land. In our minds, this now confirmed that nothing could stop our European escapade.

Jackson and I woke up around noon. I tried to piece together the previous night, but it wasn't a good time for such a complicated task.

"Jackson, we're going to the top of the mountain today. You ready?"

"What are you talking about? My head is killing me."

"The shrooms, brother. Today is the day. Let's go to the train station."

I went to the kitchen to get Jackson a Coke. Then I reached deep in my bag and pulled out the psychedelic drug. Jackson had never eaten mushrooms before, and this stuff was the real deal. I was so excited; I convinced Jackson nothing could go wrong. Both of us took quick showers, locked the door, and headed to the subway.

When we got to the main train station, I made sure Jackson was right by my side. There was no way were going to have another debacle like we did on the way to Amsterdam. I was tempted to hold his hand just to make sure. We boarded a train heading south to Rottach-Egern. We would have to take a couple of different trains to get there, but we had become familiar with the transportation system by now. We sat side by side in the middle of one of the train cars. Jackson's hangover subsided, and it was replaced by curiosity.

"Cam, so what are these mushrooms going to be like?"

"It's going to change your life, man. These are probably pretty strong so we have to try to stay calm. If it starts getting too intense, just try to breathe."

"All right. I'm just going to trust you with this."

"We are going to eat an awesome lunch and take them right before we go up the mountain."

The train ride south was stimulating. The countryside was full of wildflower fields, rushing brooks, and dense forests. It was overcast, and it rained sporadically during the ride. I was excited, but I also felt collected. I was mentally readying myself for the event. It was the calm before the storm.

Our final train came to a squeaky stop in Rottach-Egern. Jackson and I stepped off the train, and we were already in the middle of town. As I exited the doors of the train station, I took two steps and looked up to the right. There it was, Wallberg Mountain, all 5,200 feet of it. It shot straight up through the low clouds. It was two o'clock in the afternoon, and I was starving.

I saw an old man walking his dog on the sidewalk. I had to try my German one more time. "Wo ist der beste restaurant?" (Where is the best restaurant?)

"The Messner Gütl, Kirchenwirt, Seestrasse 53 in Rottach-Egern. Das Haus gibt es schon über 300 Jahren. Essen die Enten." (Messner Gütl. The house is over 300 years old. Eat the duck.)

"Ich danke Ihnen. Haben einen guten tag." (Thank you. Have a good day.)

Jackson and I made our way to the historic restaurant. The rooms were very cozy and rustic, with a beautiful fireplace. There was also a terrace with a view of Lake Ternsee. We took a seat in the corner. Since it was the middle of the afternoon, the place was not crowded.

Jackson and I both ordered the duck l'orange with braised red cabbage and a glass of French red wine from Cotes-du-Rhone. The meal was important, and it felt okay to blow it out for the occasion. We tried to act sophisticated, but all that went out the window by the end of the meal.

"Jackson, how is your duck?"

"It's incredible. The wine is perfect for it."

"All right, Chef Boyardee." I reached in my pocket and took out the mushrooms. "Put this on your plate. Just pretend like it's part of the meal."

I split up the shrooms and threw half on Jackson's plate. We both ate all of it and washed it down with our second glass of wine. It wasn't exactly the perfect compliment to the cuisine. It was super sketchy, but I wanted to time it right. The next cable car was traveling up the mountain in thirty minutes. I was afraid of heights, and I wanted to make the climb before the drug took full effect.

Jackson and I paid the bill, and we headed to the lift for the epic climb. I walked up to buy a ticket for the ride, but it was full. Fuck. Things were starting to get a little warped, and the next ride was not for another twenty minutes. After waiting another ten minutes, I realized that I completely underestimated the potency of these mushrooms.

I looked over at Jackson, and his eyes looked like they were about to pop out of his head. He was wearing a green Adidas shirt. Somebody's cell phone went off, and the tiered logo on Jackson's shirt danced to the sound of the ringtone. The next car pulled up, and it was time to go to the top of the mountain.

"I don't know if I can fit in that thing, Cam. It's so small. It looks like a pool ball."

I just looked up at the mountain. "Holy shit. Breathe, man. Breathe."

We both hesitated but got inside of the gondola. There were six other people inside with us. In no time, it started to be pulled upward by the thick cable on top.

The first part of the ride was bearable. I knew it took twenty-five minutes to get to the peak. But the drug was just too powerful. I was absolutely terrified of heights. The wind made the gondola swing, and I swore I wouldn't look out the window. Jackson had a different perspective.

"Cam, check out the lake. It's so blue. Come look."

I hesitated but agreed. I peeked out the window as we continued the climb. I held the gaze for a couple of moments, and then, it really hit me. I started to sweat, and I felt extremely nauseous. The storm had come.

I ripped off my shirt and sat down in the corner. Grabbing my knees, I rocked back and forth, trying to comfort myself. It didn't help. Then, I couldn't hold it anymore. Puke spewed from my mouth and into the corner of the condensed space. Remember that we had six other passengers with us.

"Cam! Cam! Are you dying, man? Jesus Christ. That smells awful."

"It's the duck, dude. It's the duck."

Very soon after, Jackson threw up on the floor too. Both of our releases made the psychedelic trip even more intense. I laid in the fetal position the rest of the ride up. Thank God it only took five more minutes.

The people we were with were shocked, to say the least. Fortunately, we were in a small German town, and my behavior may have seemed strange, but it also just looked like I was extremely sick.

When the gondola stopped at the top, two women followed us out to help. They ran inside to the beer garden and got us some water. We thanked them, and then I put my shirt back on backward and inside out just like the night before.

Jackson and I downed the water, and we began to feel better. The clouds began to subside, and the sun shown through in small rays. I soon realized we were on the top of a mountain. We made it.

After sitting on a bench for an hour, we rallied. It was time to get a beer. We went inside the beer garden and ordered a couple of tall Bavarian beers. We found a seat with a perfect view. It was a lively site. The sun began to fully emerge. The rays streamed over the top of the surrounding peaks. The gray rocky faces melted into the green trees below, and those colors rolled down, funneling into the lake.

The spot was popular for hang gliders as well. We saw three of them floating down from where we were sitting. They were yellow, red, and pink. They soared and left streaks of their bright colors behind them. It was beautiful as the streaks intertwined in the sky.

As we sat there overlooking Lake Ternsee and the Alps sipping on Bavarian beer, I felt free. It had been a rocky road up the mountain for sure, but I was at peace as I sat in that beer garden. I couldn't help but think of David Bowie's "It Ain't Easy":

When you climb to the top of the mountain
Look out over the sea
Think about the places perhaps, where a young man could be.

Now, was I really free at the time? It's hard to say. I wasn't completely self-sufficient, so in that respect, I was tied down by something. My thoughts raced.

I was in conflict in many different ways. I despised the people who sat in coffee shops and listened to music that nobody had ever heard of just to be different. They would talk to you about the meaning of life in a heartbeat, and that always got on my nerves.

I was also bored by the people who couldn't ever dig deeper than the surface, the true superficiality that pervades adolescent life. I knew folks who had to be seen with the right people, wearing the right clothes, and driving the right car. I still don't understand why people put such emphasis on those things. How many Lily dresses, Air Force Ones, or Costa Del Mars do people need to be satisfied? All of these thoughts swirled around in my head as I watched the sun cascade over the mountains.

While on top of that mountain, I figured out that I should live my life from the inside out. If I wasn't happy on the inside, what was the point of pretending to be happy on the outside? How could I derive joy from outside things if it didn't reside deep within me?

Now, understanding how to obtain this peace was more of a challenge than I realized. Idealizing such things was different than realizing them.

It would take quite some time before I understood how to become a free individual. I coasted along, thinking I was free for longer than needed.

Were drinking and doing drugs the way to freedom? At the time, I thought it was a channel that accompanied the lifestyle. This hallucinogenic state I was in made me feel incredible, and I concluded that reaching those momentary highs were important in life, whatever form they came in. I didn't realize that the route I was taking was putting more chains on me.

The gondola was making its last trip back down, so it was time to leave this immaculate place. Jackson and I boarded with fewer people than before, and we maintained our composure as we descended. The further away we got from the top, we somehow came down from the nirvana we had obtained. The town below became bigger and bigger, and we had to reenter the world from which we had escaped momentarily. Could I embrace the realizations I had at the top and live them out at the bottom? Only time would tell.

I pondered these epiphanies for the whole train ride back to Munich. I was absorbed in internal dialogues, leaving Jackson to his own accord. This psychedelic trip was not as interactive as my first one but much more introspective. When I was on top of that mountain, everything seemed to fall in place. I had a direction, a motive, a purpose.

This was a huge stepping-stone in my continuous search for something. I had to live my life with reason. There were things further down the road that solidified this desire and gave me strength to carry out my wishes. This was the tip of the iceberg in a lot of ways. It eventually made me repeatedly ask, "What am I doing?" and "Why am I doing it?"

I believe that experience only planted a seed. It's understandable that my life wouldn't change instantaneously. I didn't even know if it was going to change at all. We still had four days left in Germany. To address this issue with only four days left in the trip was too much for me. Like in times past, I pushed the idea away.

Socializing that night was not an option. When Jackson and I made it back to the apartment, the effects of the mushrooms were waning, and we were both drained. I couldn't really conceptualize my experience just yet, so it was hard to convey what I thought.

I'm not sure what kind of experience Jackson had. We never really went into detail about it. It must have been something extreme like mine because whenever it comes up, we change the subject. Even with such a close friend, some things aren't worth discussing. Privacy is understandable.

13

I woke up around two o'clock the next afternoon after a very deep slumber. Jackson was still asleep, and there was no rush to do anything.

I sat up in bed and waved my hand in front of my face. Good, nothing weird. I was back to reality. A nice long shower sounded great. I headed to Club Van der Dookie and said hello to my first German acquaintance. Open up, buddy, here it comes.

As I sat there on the Doo Doo Slide trying to wake up, I realized this was an important day. We were having dinner with the Traugotts that night. Dr. Traugott had invited us at the beginning of the trip, and we coordinated a date that was suitable for all of us. I wondered if he would forgive me for my initial encounter with the very spot I was sitting. I knew the toilet had forgiven me, but would Dr. Traugott?

After a long shower, I came back to the big room in my towel. Jackson was standing on the porch, smoking a cigarette. He must have realized he was back to reality as well.

"Jackson, you all right?"

"Yeah. Just thinking about some stuff."

Jackson, thinking about some stuff? Was this the same guy I came on the trip with? I thought for a split second the mushrooms had really messed him up.

"Well, don't get too deep. We should go grab a beer at the Haufbrauhaus. Plus we are eating with the Traugotts tonight."

Jackson finished his last puff, and I think he understood what I was saying.

"Yeah, dude. Let's do that. I could use a beer. Dr. Traugott is going to be glad to see you."

I enjoyed the sarcastic remark. It meant Jackson hadn't completely lost his mind. I would hate for him to accidentally fry his brain.

Now, we were off to the Haufbrauhaus. This was the most famous beer garden in the world. It was founded in 1589. Fuck me running. This place was over four hundred years old. You just can't find stuff like that in the States. Damn, the United States didn't even exist back then.

Wilhelm V, Duke of Bavaria, used to have beer imported into Munich. So instead of continuing the arduous process, he decided to make his own brewery. Notably, Wilhelm V's son monopolized the production of wheat beer, and this brewery has been making the beer in Munich ever since. But enough history.

Jackson and I sat down and went to work. This beer was money in the bank. Just think about a rich, frothy, ice cold taste of heaven. The place was a little touristy, but that beer was awesome.

We sat and enjoyed the scenery, which happened to be an attractive female in front of us. There was a group of young girls and guys about our age. Overhearing their conversation, we could tell they were German. One girl kept our attention. She had a bright blue g string hanging out of her low-cut pants. Almost her whole ass was showing.

"Jackson, check out that butt floss."

"Butt floss and beer. Nice."

Perfect moment for an '80s high five. Soon after, we noticed a gentleman who had been walking around the beer garden with his camera. I just assumed he was a tourist. He was a tall man with thick glasses and dark hair. We would see a flash go off in the distance and really think nothing of it. He got close to us and turned in the direction of the butt floss.

He just stood there for about five minutes, looking through his camera. He definitely took multiple pictures of this unsuspecting girl. The guy acted like it was normal.

I was a pretty peaceful guy, but the alcohol convinced me that this creep deserved a confrontation.

I looked to my left and shouted, "Hey, you pervert! You going to go jack off to those pictures later?"

"Ce?" the man replied with a confused look.

"What kind of shitty response is that? Jackson, this guy's Spanish, and he said he was going to jack off later."

Jackson responded, "Cam, leave this guy alone."

The man turned toward us and raised both of his arms with his palms facing up saying, "Je suis en visite." (I am just visiting.)

Once I realized he was French, I was livid. I went into a tirade about our experience in France.

"Oh! You're one of those French fuckers. Because of you French assholes, we couldn't stay in a hotel, and a guy ripped us off to stay in a whorehouse!"

By this time, people at the tables close by turned our way, including the German girl with the butt floss. I felt like it was my duty to let her know about this creepy man.

"Hey, frau (miss). This French dude is taking pictures of your underwear and your nice butt. Me and my friend weren't looking at how nice your ass is though."

I thought this girl might be cool with me letting her know she was being stalked, but as it turned out, her enormous boyfriend, Hanz, thought I was hitting on her. Hanz had a bigger temper than me, and he had bigger muscles than me. Hanz was probably bigger than me in a lot of ways given the attractiveness of his girlfriend. He had also been drinking longer than me too. Hanz jumped up from his table and caught me with a left hook dead in the face, knocking me flat on my back.

As I got up to retaliate, waiters had already arrived on the scene. They grabbed me and Jackson and threw us out of the beer garden. Once out in the street, I could feel my lip swelling up.

"What's wrong with you, Cam? I know you have a temper but damn. That guy laid you out. I don't understand why you are acting so confrontational. I've never seen you get in a fight in your life.

"I don't know, man. It just happened. Those beers got the best of me, and I wasn't expecting Schwarzenegger to get in the mix. How does my lip look?"

"Like shit. What are you going to tell the Traugotts about that?"

"I will figure that out later. Let's get back and change so we aren't late."

"You like living on the edge, don't you, bud?"

"Just be quiet."

After a change of clothes, we made our way to Dr. Traugott's home. It took a long subway ride and several bus stops, but we made it in time. The house was on the outskirts of town, and when we got there, I went up to ring the doorbell.

Mrs. Traugott answered the door and welcomed us in her German accent. "Hello, welcome. Please come in and take a seat. Dinner is almost ready."

While being polite, Mrs. Traugott also did a double-take of my lip but didn't say anything else. Jackson and I went in the living room, where Dr. Traugott was sitting in a chair reading a newspaper. He put the paper down, smiled at Jackson, and then glared at me. Not a good start.

"Hello boys. Are you hungry?"

"Yes sir," we answered. We followed him to the dining room table as Mrs. Traugott put the final touches on the meal in the kitchen.

"Would you like something to drink?"

"Yes sir," we echoed. Dr. Traugott made his way over to the liquor cabinet and pulled out a bottle. This was going to sting like hell if I accepted a drink.

Dr. Traugott explained, "This is a Riesling wine from Cologne. It is the only place they make it in the world. They don't use a cork because it will ruin the wine."

Interesting fact. My busted lip could handle some wine, so I nodded and waited for him to pour. Dr. Traugott filled all of our glasses to the brim. Jackson and I thanked him for the hospitality.

Mrs. Traugott came in soon after with the meal. She had cooked baked chicken, potatoes, and white asparagus with cheese. Finally, we were all seated and ready to eat. I expected a prayer, but they just nodded for us to start. Conversation ensued, at least for Jackson.

Dr. Traugott kidded Jackson for a little bit about the Amsterdam debacle.

"Jackson, your mom called me, very worried. You must have been pretty tired not to hear the police knocking on the door."

"Yes sir. I am sorry about that."

"Oh, do not worry. I am sure you needed your rest."

As he said this, Dr. Traugott turned to me and squinted a little bit. I took a big gulp of wine. Each sip went straight into the open wound in my lip, and I cringed. Neither Dr. nor Mrs. Traugott had commented on my lip, so I just pretended like the wound was not there for the time being. Mrs. Traugott quickly refilled our glasses with the Riesling.

"Do you like the wine? I have an extra bottle for you to take with you."

I felt left out so I chimed in, "Thank you, Dr. Traugott. You have a lovely home. What kind of doctor were you?"

He responded very sternly, "I am a psychiatrist."

Dear Lord, here it comes. He had been psychoanalyzing me since we picked up our bags from the airport. Oh shit, he has been in my head the whole time. Damn you, Dr. Traugott. No wonder you didn't say anything in the bathroom that first day. You were too busy swimming in my subconscious. I took another big gulp of wine. The more drunk I got, the less the stinging hurt.

"Jackson, how is your granddad?"

"He is good. He told me you were good friends."

"Oh yes. We had many good times with your grandparents when they lived here. Please give them my best."

"Yes sir."

Alcohol was really starting to kick in for me, but I was still nervous. Mrs. Traugott filled up my glass again.

"Dr. Traugott, my granddad and Jackson's granddad were friends too. They worked on some different business projects."

Silence from everyone in the room. Awkward moments passed. Why was I speaking?

Mrs. Traugott tried to change the subject, and she asked, "Boys, do you like the food?"

Jackson and I replied in unison, "Yes ma'am."

Mrs. Traugott continued, "I am glad you made it to our home. It is outside the city, and we are able to enjoy the many walking trails."

All right, I had this one. I knew I could make a worthy contribution.

"I have heard that Germans like to enjoy nature. That is nice you can still walk around."

Silence.

Cam! You are such a fool. Shut your mouth and just listen. Pretend like you are shy. I finished another glass of wine. Mrs. Traugott filled me up again. At that point, I had an angel sitting on one shoulder and a devil on the other. The more alcohol I drank, the bigger the devil got. I managed to listen quietly for several more topics of conversation while drinking more wine.

As Jackson took the reins, anger was building inside of me. Every now and then, Dr. Traugott would look at me and let out a heavy sigh. Each time, I gave a courteous half smile exposing my swollen lip even more, but the water was beginning to boil. The seventh time he did it, I had enough.

Dr. Traugott continued, "What are your plans for the rest of the trip?"

I answered quickly "Well, Dr. Freud, first, we are going to drink the whole bottle of that Riesling you're giving us, and then we are going to chase some women!"

"Excuse me?"

The alcohol took control and all hell broke loose. "You heard me, you Nazi! Me and Jackson are going to get as drunk as possible and chase German women."

Jackson intervened but to no avail, "Cam! Shut up!"

I raised my voice, and it stayed there as I stood up. "Stay out of this, Jackson. This is between me and 'Holy Man.' Look, you old man. You have been mean mugging me since I got here. What did I ever do to you? Okay, okay. I took a shit in your bathroom. Is it really that big of a deal? You didn't have to go in there. We could have figured out the damn hot water by ourselves. It's not like it was a Nazi shower. I mean, we weren't going to die in there from poison like the Jews did! I bet you are looking at my lip too."

I pointed at it and continued to yell, "Well, a Nazi hit me today for no good reason. He was just being a fucking Nazi! You were in on all that Nazi stuff, weren't you? Weren't you? Got news for you, Dr. Traugott, America won that war. You can go to hell and tell Hitler to go fuck himself while you're down there!"

I was fuming, but then my conscience returned. Holy shit, what had I done?

Dr. Traugott sat there calmly as I finished my tirade. Mrs. Traugott had tears in her eyes. Dr. Traugott digested the whole thing. Like a good psychiatrist, he showed very little emotion in his response. I was officially a patient now due to my psychotic outburst.

"Cameron, I hold no such animosity. I suggest you take a look at your behavior. Maybe you have some unaddressed issues."

I had calmed some, but Dr. Traugott's response caused me to become irate again. I wasn't going to lose this battle.

I shouted, "Issues! Who the hell are you to tell me I have issues? This is over. Mrs. Traugott, thank you for the meal. I will be leaving now."

I excused myself from the table and walked right out of the front door toward the bus stop. The next bus was pulling up as I got there.

All the way back to the apartment, I kept laughing to myself about that one word: issues. What kind of psychobabble was that? I was here to have a good time. I just ate mushrooms and went to the top of a mountain. I was nineteen years old. What could an old man like that know that I didn't?

Unfortunately for me, I didn't have a key to the apartment. Being a drama queen did me no good whatsoever. I had to wait for Jackson to get back anyways. After about an hour, he turned the corner.

"Cam, what the fuck is wrong with you? I have never seen you get in a fight, and that was the second one today."

"Dr. Traugott was being a dick. I'm sorry, dude. I just couldn't take it anymore."

"Well, I covered for your ass. They were offended, but I just said you couldn't hold your alcohol very well, and they said it was okay. Damn, man, try to relax. By the way, they still gave us the bottle of wine."

"Shit. I'm such an idiot. Okay. I will apologize to Dr. Traugott when we get back to Ellington. For now, let's just pretend like it didn't happen."

"All right, man, whatever."

We walked upstairs, and Jackson unlocked the door. We walked into the main room, and the bottle of absinthe and the Fodor's guide were sitting on the table.

I opened up the traveler's guide and looked through nightlife for Munich. Let's see. We had already been to P1 and Kultfabrik. What was this thing here? Club Vier Tousand. I understood the name as Club 4000. It had eight dance floors. This sounded like the place to be. It was way outside of town, but it sounded like the bomb.

"All right, Jackson, hand me the absinthe."

Once in my hands, I opened the bottle and took a big swig. It hurt like the devil despite my major buzz, and I slammed my fist down on the table in pain. I passed it back to Jackson, motioning him to do the same.

'Cam, are you sure you want 150 proof alcohol on an open wound?"

"Don't worry, man. It's just sterilizing it."

"You're a fucking nut."

We continued the pattern for about four pulls. I don't really remember exactly how much we drank, truthfully.

———————————

Jackson and I traveled to the outskirts of the city to find the coveted Club 4000. We made it to the address, but there were no people around. Could the Fodor's have been outdated? I went up to the door to look inside. Maybe they were having a private party. Nope, no one there. It was about one o'clock, prime time for club entrance. Shit out of luck.

We walked back through the parking lot and had no idea how to get home. A car was pulling up not too far away, and I ran up to it. There were two German guys in their twenties.

"Hey! Hey! German guys. A Nazi punched me earlier but you guys are cool. The club is closed. Do you know another sweet spot to go party? Can we get a ride there?"

The one in the passenger seat said, "Yeah, sure, get in."

Jackson and I piled into the backseat of the little car and struck up a conversation. We hadn't smoked any weed since Geneva and hoped these guys could hook us up.

Jackson started, "You guys know where to get some grass?"

The driver looked over at his friend and smiled. "There isn't good stuff here. You need to go to Berlin. When you get off the train, there will be a short man with a long black coat under a bridge. He has everything you need."

My turn: "All right, cool, how long does it take to get to Berlin?"

Passenger's turn: "Oh, it's about a seven-hour train ride."

In my illogical thought process, I concluded, "All right, we might go there tomorrow."

I was dead serious at the time.

During the drive back toward the city, we asked about other things like the soccer matches and girls. Nothing too absurd that I recall.

They pulled up to the curb and told us we were at the club. Jackson and I thanked them time and again, one of us yelling, "Yeah, Berlin! Gonna get the good stuff soon."

This club had lasers galore. Like other places, the club was deafening with techno music. It was a small club but very crowded. Then I saw her on the lower dance floor: the woman of my dreams, the biggest girl in the club.

I poked Jackson and said, "Watch this, I'm going to snag that chick over there."

"Are you kidding?"

"No, she is all mine."

Honestly, this girl was somewhere in between the size of the girl who turns into a blueberry in Willy Wonka and a beach ball. I found her on the dance floor and starting making my move. In that moment, I just wanted to make the trip even more memorable. Drinking made me do some strange things, and this was no exception. I know it's wrong in retrospect, but I would eventually get what I deserved in the long run.

I pointed at her, and she started to smile. Songs went by, and I used different mating calls in the form of dance. I clapped my hands and spun around. I grabbed her by the hand and spun her around. I waved my arms in front of my face and swung my hips like Forrest Gump teaching Elvis how to dance.

Soon, we got closer and closer. Every once in a while, I would look up to find Jackson staring in disbelief. I gave him the thumbs up and slapped her on the ass, and he cracked up each time.

Oh, but she got the best of me that night. After breaking a sweat from the fast-paced songs, I moved in for the kill. My mouth moved toward her to initiate the first kiss. Landed it. Great start. We continued to make out in the middle of the crowd, and I thought it was a lock. I started to whisper sweet nothings in her ear.

"Come on, baby, let's get out of here. I will make you feel incredible."

"No."

"You need to be with a real man."

"No."

You are like a dream come true. The night is calling us."

"No."

Was Miss Piggy really turning me down? I'll be damned if this would happen to me. Granted, my lines sounded like they came from an acne-filled preteen with braces, but I had to have a chance with this girl. I also had a nasty fat lip, which she had already kissed multiple times. I thought if she wasn't afraid of AIDS, then she would surely come home with me.

Jackson was still laughing at me while he was dancing with several attractive girls. After many attempts, I gave up. I just got turned down by the fattest girl in the club. Great ego boost, Cam. You really are a stud.

I pulled Jackson aside and slurred, "That girl won't leave with me."

"I thought you were the self-proclaimed ladies man. Gah, you are a loser! Plus your lip is nasty."

"Look, man . . . look, man. It's just a cold streak. It's like basketball; you just got to keep shooting."

"You are ridiculous."

I drowned my sorrows with some shots as the bar was closing. I had been in Europe for just over two weeks, and Jackson was getting all the ass. What the hell was going on? Maybe I had overestimated my skills while with Tar Heel women. I mean, it is 65 percent girls up there, so the ratio was definitely in my favor. This would not be the end of my quest. I would score. Oh yes, I would.

14

The morning passed by once again, and I awoke well past noon.
Given we were at the World Cup, it was probably a good idea to watch
some soccer for a change. I had to support the Red, White, and Blue for
the tournament. The American team hadn't done too well so far, and this
was disappointing given their surprising success in the last World Cup in
South Korea.

In group play, the United States had lost to the Czech Republic 3-0
and tied Italy 1-1. Today, we played Ghana. If we won, there was a chance
of us going through to the next round.

Jackson actually woke me up for a change. He threw a sock at my face
from his bed. "Hey, hippo hunter. Time to get up."

It took me a second to register the cut down, and then I just shook my
head. "Wow, did I really do that last night? This absinthe stuff is starting
to mess with me."

"No, dude. You should definitely keep it up. You're a pimp."

"Just be quiet, dickhead."

Jackson and I traveled back to the fan zone set up at Olympic Park.
The game was at four o'clock, and we arrived somewhere around three.
There was a big screen set up, and different tents for drinks. Our odd
choice of drink for the afternoon: Mojitos. Yes, they were being served in
Munich for some reason.

Settling in close to the screen, Jackson and I took a seat in the open grassy area. A black man from Ghana was sitting behind us. He was sitting Indian style with a red jersey on and a bucket hat with his country's flag. His eyes were bloodshot.

I turned around and held my hand to my mouth like I was smoking a joint while saying, "Hey man, you smoka da ganja?"

And no, he wasn't Jamaican so I don't know why I said that.

He didn't know much English, and he just laughed. Then these three fucking German assholes came on the scene. The game was about to start, and they took a seat right behind us. They were plastered and obnoxious to say the least. I kept quiet because they reminded me of Hanz.

The game began. The US looked slack, and Ghana was putting on the pressure. Every errant American pass was accompanied by an outlandish comment by the Germans behind us.

"Oh, the US plays fairy soccer."

Not even close to being cool.

Then, in the twenty-second minute, one of our players passed it back to the captain, Claudio Reyna. Well, he lost the ball, and Ghana scored on a breakaway. Reyna also got hurt on the play. Great display by the US.

"Oh, look how wimpy Americans are. They are like fairies."

Jackson was starting to show his Irish temper again. "Man, shut the fuck up and watch the game."

"Oh, touchy American."

Jackson looked at me and said, "I need some more liquor for this shit."

Right before the half, Demarcus Beasley, a US winger, intercepted the ball and played it across the box to Clint Dempsey, and Dempsey nailed it into the back of the net. 1-1, and Jackson and I were jumping, screaming, and high fiving.

Jackson was very passionate about the US team, and he looked back at the Germans.

"Fuck you, Nazis! We are winning this shit!"

I bit my lip to test for pain and kept silent. Somehow, the attitude of animosity had shifted from me to Jackson. Maybe I had set a bad example. Or maybe it was the Mojitos. Things started feeling very ominous.

Tension was rising. Just a few minutes later, Ghana exploited the weakness of the American team. A US defender cleared the ball straight up from our corner into our box. Then, big goofy American defender

Oguchi Onyewu fouled a Ghana player, and it resulted in a penalty kick. It was a pretty shitty call, but that's how the game goes sometimes. Ghana scored, and it was 2-1 at half.

The second half went a little better. We hit the post on a header and had another header go just over the crossbar. By the seventy-fifth minute, we knew the game was over. Jackson and I turned to the Ghana man and gave him the thumbs up.

The three Germans were leaving, but not without Jackson standing to give them a Nazi salute and saying, "Heil Hitler, bitches!"

One of the Germans, the smallest of the three, turned around and glared at Jackson.

"Did you just say Heil Hitler?"

"Yeah. I said bitches too," Jackson shouted back.

This turned out to be a touchy subject. The smaller German quickly became violent. The response was very different from Dr. Traugott and similar to Hanz.

The small German charged Jackson, but Jackson threw him on the ground. Jackson hopped on the German and was about to start throwing punches. I rushed to try and break it up, but it was too late. One of the other Germans tackled me while the third one pulled Jackson off the little man.

My German opponent was feisty. I managed to get back on my feet and tried to calm him down.

I said slowly, "Look, brother. Germany is cool. We have had a great . . ."

He sent a right jab straight into my grill. Mother of God! Why did he have to hit me there?

Then, Ghana came to the rescue. The peaceful man in the red jersey had already broken up Jackson and the other two. For my sake, he got in between me and the third German too.

The Ghana man was yelling in his native African tongue. The strange language caused everyone within twenty yards to stop what they were doing.

By the time the Ghana man finished lecturing us with noises and clicks I had never heard before, the soccer match had ended. It was official. The US was out of the tournament. Jackson and I looked at each other and decided to go downtown to start the night early.

————————

Once in the middle of town, we actually found an Australian bar. It was named Ned Kelly's after the famous outlaw. It was in a basement, and there was a large sign on the wall reading:

He was an outlaw,
He was a killer,
He was our hero . . .

He wore a bucket on his head!

Jackson and I had no idea what this was all about, but we quickly found out that Australians were mighty cool folk.

For some reason, I was wearing a green shirt and Jackson had on a yellow one. These were the colors of the Australian uniforms. We were running out of clean clothes, and these were among the last clean items we had. Big coincidence on the scene. Don't worry. For the US game, we had flags and other American things, but due to the horrendous play of our country, my American support ended when the whistle blew.

"Jackson, let's pretend we are Australian."

"What? Like 'Put another shrimp on the barbie'?"

"Yeah, except we are not at Outback Steakhouse."

"Oh, you're right, genius; we are at Ned Kelly's, where 'he wore a bucket on his head.'"

I knew Jackson was pissed about the game, so I let the sarcasm slide. He was starting to get on my nerves a little bit. I wasn't too happy about being hit in the mouth again. I tried to let the whole incident fade away. We chose to forget about it and enjoy the night.

We ordered some sandwiches and drank a lot of Fosters. It was all they had on tap. I have actually heard that Australians hate Fosters, but whatever. Australia was playing Croatia at nine o'clock, and the place began to fill up with rowdy fans.

In the second minute, Croatia scored on a beautiful free kick. I have never heard so much profanity in my life. So we just figured we would join in with them.

"Fucking crikey, mate."

"Ah, gator shit!"

"Outback fucking Steakhouse!"

One of the Australian forwards got rugby tackled in the penalty box. No call. More outrage.

"Ned Kelly's gonna slit yer Croatian throats."

"Ah, kanga shit!"

In the middle of the first half, Australia got a penalty kick. The player buried it, and that tiny basement went absolutely nuts. It was crazy. They started chanting as well. Anybody would yell out the first three words, and the whole bar would finish it.

"Aussie! Aussie! Aussie!"

"Oy! Oy! Oy!"

"Aussie! Aussie! Aussie!"

"Oy! Oy! Oy!"

Halftime. More drinks were passed around. Everybody there was throwing back Fosters like there was no tomorrow. The second half started.

Croatia took a shot in the fifty-sixth minute, and the Australian keeper screwed up, letting the ball in the net. More profanities that could scar a child for life. But Australia kept fighting for the match. After some missed opportunities, the seventy-ninth minute provided hope.

A ball was played in, there was a scramble in the box, and an Aussie banged it home. Pandemonium ensued from the citizens of the Land Down Under. The last ten minutes were extremely tense. Both teams were trying to advance past group stage. If Australia held on to the tie, they would go through.

That last ten minutes, things just got mean. There were three red cards, two for Croatia and one for Australia. That was the passion that made this game great. It was really ruthless, and I loved it. The Australians fended off countless attacks from the Croatians. The whistle blew, and Australia was going to the next round. Fans were running on the field, and the referee was pushing players off of him. It was extraordinary.

Immediately, the whole bar stormed up the stairs and out into the street. A crowd of about forty people jumped up and down together and chanted that familiar phrase:

"Aussie! Aussie! Aussie!"

"Oy! Oy! Oy!"

"Aussie! Aussie! Aussie!"

"Oy! Oy! Oy!"

Jackson and I were right in the middle of it. I don't know how long it lasted, but I was jacked. I even started leading one of the chants. I screamed the first part:

"Aussie! Aussie! Aussie!"

Forty people responded, "Oy! Oy! Oy!"

Talk about a high. This was all natural, minus the immense alcohol. Nevertheless, things were just absurd. Jackson and I hung around, still pretending to be Australian. We roamed the streets, having no plan in mind. We spent that night with true fans. I couldn't really tell you if we went to a bar or not.

I do remember sitting on a large fountain with a bottle of liquor that came from God knows where. A skinny black guy was sitting next to us. All of a sudden, a fight broke out on the lower part of the square. This guy got cracked in the head with a beer bottle. Jackson and I were pretty out of it, so we just kind of stared in amazement. This guy got his ass whipped while I tried to avoid any kind of confrontation.

Out of nowhere, the black guy sitting next to us broke our bottle of liquor and pointed it at me. I was way too drunk by that point to react aggressively. I brushed him off, figuring that he probably had more alcohol than blood in his system. The next thing I knew, I woke up to light streaming through a small spot in the curtains of the apartment. I rolled over and went back to sleep until three in the afternoon.

———————————

Jackson was out cold. I woke up first once again. I was proud to wake up at three o'clock instead of three thirty like my lazy friend. We lounged around the apartment for another hour or so, our stomachs growling louder and louder. Chugging Coke, club soda, and water wasn't good enough. I had to eat something.

Guido's wasn't going to do it this time. This empty belly needed a real meal. There was an Italian restaurant right across the street, and Jackson and I went there to eat. The table was full of pasta and bread, a perfect solution to satisfy the appetite. The bartender was extremely friendly, and he sent over some after dinner shots in gratitude for our money spent. I guess they weren't getting too much business and wanted customers to return. Jackson and I took them down, and we walked back to the apartment.

Okay. Our flight was leaving on Sunday at seven o'clock in the morning. It was Friday, and we wanted to make it to Club 4000. I put on some more music, and Jackson I sat around the apartment again. What do you know, there was still some absinthe left. The bottle was a little less than halfway gone. In our vast intelligence, we started drinking it again.

Like before, we coupled it with vodka in between. We also had some beer to wash it down. For God's sake, you think we would have taken it easy for a change. This was just not in the cards. There was no casual drinking involved. It was just straight to the face. Time passed by quickly.

By eleven o'clock, we were good and ready to go out. Jackson and I made it to the outskirts of town and reached the front door of Club 4000 once again. There were no people around; it was closed again. Damn you, Fodor's. When is the place ever going to open?

Instead of getting in a sketchy car, we saw a group of guys walking down the sidewalk. I got close enough for them to hear me.

"Hey, German guys! You heading to a club?"

"Yes. It is right around the corner. Come with us."

Even in my nebulous haze, it seemed kind of strange that they were so willing to invite two strangers with them. There were six of them, and we joined in for the short walk to the next club. I had no idea what this one was going to be like.

I was reluctant, given our past two encounters with Germans, but these guys were actually really friendly. I started talking to a guy with short gelled hair and glasses. He had a tight black shirt on with tight jeans as well.

"So where are we going?" I asked.

"It is a club in an abandoned train station. You will love it."

"Awesome. So what are you doing in Munich?"

"Oh, we came for an engineering competition. We came in second, and we are going to celebrate."

"Ah . . . you Germans and your engineering."

All of us walked across a bridge over some railroad tracks below. We could hear music coming from this large building at the bottom. They weren't shitting us. This really was an abandoned train station.

I got up to the door, and there was a ten Euro cover. No problem with that. Jackson and I went up to the bar, and all of the shots cost just one Euro. Perfect combination. Saving money and getting wasted. I ordered some tequila shots, and we threw them back.

This club was enormous. There had to have been three hundred and fifty people there, and there was still plenty of room. The music wasn't just techno. Jackson and I were in a great mood, and it was time to go hunting again. Except this time, I would search for something of higher caliber than the night before. Personality is a great quality, but I was also nineteen years old with raging hormones. I wanted to be with a pretty girl, simple as that.

Jackson and I made our way to an elevated stage, where about thirty people were dancing. We eyed two cute girls about ten feet away. The Red Hot Chili Peppers' "Dani California" came on, and everyone in there started grooving. This was when the song was brand new.

Getting born in the state of Mississippi
Papa was a copper and mama was a hippie
In Alabama she would swing a hammer
Price you gotta pay when you break the panorama

Jackson nudged me. "We should go talk to those girls."

Cocky and dumb, I responded, "No man, play it cool. They will come to us."

The plan did not work out. We hesitated, and we were dead. The girls ended up walking away very shortly after. Oh well, there were hundreds of other girls there.

Jackson and I went back to the huge bar; and on the way, I saw comedic genius. There was a very good-looking girl dancing with a guy in a wheelchair. He would roll back and forth, and she would shake her ass in his face. She even gave him some sort of lap dance. Quite humorous. I had to give it to the handicapped man, he was doing better than me.

Jackson and I grabbed some beers and headed outside. I was hungry again, and they were serving sausages. I quickly grabbed one and slabbed some mustard on it. It didn't take long for me to spill it all over my shirt. Not soon after my purchase, Jackson went missing. Not the end of the world but of some concern.

The outside area was strange. There was sand all over the ground. It was some type of beach theme. I looked around, and over in the corner, I saw something that was simply astonishing. A large group of guys were dancing with themselves. This included our engineering friends and Jackson. I ran up to him with my half-eaten sausage.

"Jackson, are you fucking dancing with gay guys?"

"Yeah, man. The engineering guys asked me to dance. I want to see if I get hit on."

"Are you out of your . . ."

Midsentence, a man in a silver sequin shirt grabbed my shoulder and said to me, "That sausage looks yummy. Come dance."

I responded very sarcastically, "Sorry bud. You're shirt is outstanding and your dance moves are incredible, but I have another man waiting for me inside."

Jackson was pretty out of it, so it didn't take long to convince him to leave the gay scene. He was really starting to get on my nerves. I think I was sexually frustrated as well. Knowing that even guys were hitting on my formerly inexperienced friend was pissing me off. Despite my initial reaction, I was able to brush it off momentarily and spend the rest of the night trying to enjoy this club.

Nevertheless, Jackson and I had been together almost nonstop for about two and a half weeks. Anybody can get annoying after that. I'm sure there were things I was doing that bothered Jackson as well. The discrepancy in the amount of tail obtained between the two of us was becoming a topic of debate.

"Don't get jealous, Cam. Even gay guys are into me."

"Are you serious? You really think you have a better chance hooking up than I do?"

"Let the numbers speak for themselves, my friend."

"Damn you. I'm going to hook up with a chick tonight just to prove you wrong."

My pride was in full force. In my stubbornness, I would not be outdone. The rest of the evening, I was trying to pick up every girl in sight. Considering this was an international gathering, some of my attempts were less than stellar.

"What's up, baby?"

"Como?" (What?)

"Oh cool, Spanish. Mi pene in los pantalones." (My penis in your pants)

Slap in the face and a no-go. On to the next girl.

"I want to be on you."

"Shen me?" (What?)

"Oh yeah, Asian talk. Ching chow, me fung wang ni."

She walked away immediately. At least she wasn't violent. Then, I saw an attractive Arabic chick. This was a lock for sure.

"Turbans are for losers. I won't make you live in a cave."

"Hal beemkani mosa'adatuk?" (Can I help you?)

"Oh sweet, Middle Eastern. Dirka dirka jihad shalom."

She threw her drink on me. My success rate was dwindling mighty fast. I was now red in the face from an aggressive Latino, given the evil eye by a small Asian, and soaked from a Middle Eastern woman. After sitting down for a moment, I came to the frank realization that I needed to stop being an asshole and find someone who spoke English. More attempts ensued with no luck. I made my way back over to my American friend.

"Any luck, player?" Jackson said sarcastically.

"I think it's time for me to leave. I'll pick up something strange on the way home."

In an extremely sarcastic voice, the overused phrase emerged, "You the man."

In our second-to-last night of European exploration, Jackson and I made our way onto the subway toward the apartment. I sat down, and there were three girls in the front of the train. Jackson was actually somewhat encouraging me while also making fun of me.

"Go for those girls up there. They won't be able to resist you."

I was degraded by this point. "They're all yours."

I waited on the train and built up courage to talk to these girls. Why it was such a daunting task, I had no idea. Maybe I was too drunk at the time. Our stop arrived; I stood up and waved at those cute girls while grabbing my crotch.

"You know you want it," I slurred.

Big surprise to everyone reading, it was unsuccessful. I stepped off the train and waited on the platform. In my frenzy and final attempt, I stared down the girls in the subway car. Gracefully, I hurled my body at the window. Then, my leg slid down between the platform and the train. Jackson had already walked off. Even in such a dire situation, I was still determined to pick up the girls. It's good to be persistent, but this was unbelievable. I tried to pull myself up, but I was stuck. The train was about to take off, most likely ripping my right leg clear off in the process.

My life didn't flash before my eyes because my cognition was at a minimum due to the intake of alcohol. Miraculously, my body began to rise from the dangerous position. Someone grabbed me underneath my arms and pulled me out into safety. I just lay on the platform to gather my thoughts. As I got into a seated position, I looked around but didn't recognize a soul.

It was time to dust myself off and try to laugh it off. That's what I did in every other situation. I ran to catch up to Jackson, who was in the distance.

"Dude, I almost lost my leg."

"What? You are so dumb. Could you be any stupider?"

Wrong thing to say at the wrong time. Like I snapped at the "Holy Man," I unleashed my anger. I sunk my fist deep into Jackson's chest as hard as I could.

"Fuck you, man, I almost died."

"You need to chill out, Cam."

"No, motherfucker."

I jumped on Jackson and wrestled him to the ground. He put up a damn good fight. We were releasing all of the pent-up aggression that had built over the trip. This drunken battle took place in the middle of an empty subway station. A couple of good punches were thrown, but it basically got to a point where we were at a stalemate. We rolled around on the ground for a couple more minutes and quit. We got up at the same time, cussing without regard.

"I should have never come on this trip with you, Cam. I never knew you were such a prick."

"You're a piece of shit."

"Fuck you."

"Oh, big words from a big brain. I'm through with you."

I turned around and ignored the rest of the slander coming from Jackson's mouth. As I got to the bottom of the apartment building, I was keyless again. I had to wait on my former opponent to open the door. Jackson came soon after, and we walked inside and went to bed silently.

15

Saturday, June 24. I had rolled around in bed for about thirty minutes, but I couldn't sleep any longer. I sat up and looked over at Jackson, who was still sleeping. It took me a moment, but the fight from hours ago as well as my cheating death replayed in my mind.

This was the last day of our trip, and I concluded that all of the stuff from last night wasn't worth it. Jackson was right. I did need to relax. In an effort to make the trip unforgettable, I had also turned into a control freak. I had been giving out orders about what we were going to do at almost every turn for the last three weeks.

I didn't do it intentionally, but I had been pretty demonstrative. Given Jackson's easy-going temperament, it worked out fine for the majority of the trip. The aggravation that developed after spending twenty days with just one other person came to fruition with our fight. I grabbed a cigarette and went out on the balcony.

I came back inside, and Jackson let out a big stretch while still in bed. He was awake.

"Did we fight last night, Cam?"

"We sure did. I kicked your ass."

"Whatever, man." Jackson paused for a moment. His hangover had set in, and it took him a couple of moments to construct his next sentence. "Dude, you could have died last night."

We couldn't help it. Jackson and I just laughed. It was a pretty serious situation but somehow we found humor in it.

"Yeah . . . That would have sucked. Let's forget about all that stuff and call a truce."

"That's fine with me. No hard feelings. We're just fightin' Irish anyways."

"True as the sky is blue. So this is our last day in Europe. What do you want to do?"

"I don't know, man. Maybe we should go to a museum. Something low key for sure."

"All right. Check out the Fodor's and pick one out. The Slide is calling me."

With little effort, Jackson found an aviation museum. We thought about going to Dachau, the World War II concentration camp. By no means were we being disrespectful, but we decided today wasn't a good day to see such horrible things.

The day passed quickly, and Jackson and I were already thinking about the night ahead. Hunger set in, but I decided to go to an Internet café first and check my bank account. I sat down, opened my online banking site, and shook my head. I only had one hundred dollars left. This equated to about eighty Euros. Jackson was completely out of money, and he realized that he had actually overdrafted several times. Our plane was leaving at seven the next morning, and I knew we would have to take a taxi to the airport. That would cost a solid forty Euros at least. I had one hundred American dollars, but it wasn't like I could exchange it right away. This left us with roughly twenty Euros apiece to blow on our last night. This was going to be tricky.

We concluded that we would give Club 4000 one last shot. We grabbed our last pizza of the trip and ate it at the apartment. The total amount of cash for the night decreased by ten Euros. Both of us decided to rest for a bit before the last hurrah. My familiar alarm went off around nine o'clock.

Luckily, there was some alcohol left in the apartment. This included the small bottle of Riesling, some vodka, and about a fourth of the bottle of absinthe. I was almost desperate enough to huff some cleaning supplies (no, not really).

We decided to drink everything but the absinthe. Jackson dug in his bag and pulled out a flask. We poured the absinthe in the flask until it was full and drank the very last sips of our newfound friend. This had to be the night that Club 4000 was open.

We walked the couple of blocks from the subway toward the enormous club. I heard music and saw people. It was open, and I was filled with joy. Finally, the damn thing was not closed.

Jackson and I stood in a long line that started at the bottom and rose up a flight of stairs. We got to the entrance, and there was a ten Euro entry. This left us with five Euros apiece for the whole night. Awesome. I could probably buy a beer to drink besides the absinthe.

I walked inside the front door at 12:30, and I quickly realized we had reached the Mecca. Right in front of me, there was an enormous dance floor with dense fog, blinding strobes, and intense lasers. Much to my surprise, this was just one room, actually just one floor. Jackson and I decided to finish off the absinthe in the bathroom. We hid in a stall and took turns gulping down the last of it. We emerged into the mayhem and joined the vigorous crowd.

While in the techno room, I couldn't tell if I was hallucinating from the absinthe or shocked by the lights. Probably both. The entire room would go pitch black while a song was building momentum. When it hit that heavy bass, a succession of intense strobes lit up the room for about a second. I jumped up and down, and I saw Jackson's movement in flashes. One moment he was to left, then to the right. One moment, hands up. Next moment, hands down. All of this was happening without the connecting motions to complete that kind of movement. I was having quite a good time.

After breaking a good sweat, we needed a breather and a drink. We walked downstairs to one of the many bars. Jackson turned to his left, and she was there. The hottest girl of the whole trip was five feet away. Jackson walked up to talk to her. Her name was Margarita, and she was from Croatia. Jackson tried some moves, but she wanted him to buy her a drink. He was completely out of money, with beer in hand, trying to think of a plan.

"You need buy me drink," the Croatian demanded.

"I can't buy you a drink. I got robbed today."

"I must leave now."

"No, no. You're the hottest girl here. Come with me."

Jackson kept trying with Margarita, and I went to explore the rest of the club. That's what happens when you're around a really hot girl. It is easy to mess it up. I knew Jackson didn't have a chance with her. But like me, he was very determined when it came to those kinds of things. He told me all about it later.

I made my way around to two large doors. I opened them up to hear these words at full blast:

Why do you build me up (Build me up)
Buttercup baby just to let me down (Let me down)
And mess me around.

There was an oldies room in the middle of the club. I was at a loss of words. I couldn't count the number of times I had shagged to beach music in the last year. For those not from the South, it is a blast. You grab the girl by the hips, spin her around, do pretzels and dips, and basically act like you are in the late fifties. It is the key to a girl's heart.

I'm not going to lie. I was a damn good dancer of the shag. This kind of dancing was my expertise. Word of advice to the doubters: If you ever come to the South, learn how to shag. It is the ultimate turn-on, especially if a girl doesn't know how to do it. You can guide them along the way, and they feel like you're the best teacher in the world. This room in Munich was perfect. The song finished, and the Temptations' "My Girl" started.

I've got sunshine
On a cloudy day.
When it's cold outside,
I've got the month of May.

I grabbed a girl and pulled her onto the dance floor. She was a good-looking German girl with dark-hair.

"You ever shagged before?" I yelled over the music.

She responded shyly, "No."

"Well, you're about to learn."

I pulled out every trick in the book. I spun her around like there was no tomorrow. We danced for a good forty-five minutes. Her eyes lit up, and we had an awesome time. After we were both good and sweaty, it was time to go grab a seat. She was still in awe.

"Where did you learn to dance so crazy?"

"The American South."

"I like it so much."

I leaned over, and we began kissing. I moved in on her neck, and she wrapped her arms around me. Just to tease her, I pulled back and waited for her to ask for more. In that moment, I saw Jackson sitting across the room by himself. I told my new German lover to hold on a minute. I made my way over to where Jackson was sitting.

"Dude, why are you sitting by yourself? This place is awesome."

"Me and Margarita went to go smoke out of a hookah. I think I just smoked some hash. I am super stoned."

"Well, you're on your own tonight, man. I'm going to take care of business."

"Okay."

I left Jackson staring and went back to my female friend. I grabbed her and we went to a different part of the club. There was a room that was playing rap. We continued to grope each other throughout the night and made it back to the oldies room. It was time to close the deal.

I started by saying, "Let's go back to my place."

"I can't."

"Yes, you can. I know you want to."

"I do want to but . . ."

"But what?"

"My mom is here with me."

"Are you shitting me?"

"No."

She pointed over to the corner to another dark-haired stylish woman. I could see where this girl got her looks from. Her mom was a total MILF. I guess Mommy and daughter were having a night out on the town. This mom was an obstacle, but I would overcome it.

"Go tell her you want to stay a little longer. Then we can sneak back to your place when she is asleep. She can cook me breakfast in the morning."

"She will never believe me."

"Come to my place then.

"My mom will know."

"Just go tell her you'll be home soon."

After much persistence, my German girl went and told her mom she would stay a little longer. The MILF left soon after. As hard as I tried, my German girl wouldn't go anywhere but back to her house. That meant I was coming with her. We walked out of the club at four o'clock. All right, Cam, flight home is in three hours, this is possible.

I snuck into her house, and we ended up in her bed. After more intimacy, I did the dirty with her. Her mom was in the other room. I looked over at the clock, and it was 5:15.

I kissed my German girl good-bye and told her a bunch of lines about how I was going to miss her. She was pretty good in bed, so I probably would miss her a little bit. I snuck back out of the house and ran to the subway.

———————————

I never traveled so fast in my life. Going full speed the whole time, I was back at the apartment in no time. I banged on the door.

"Jackson!" I screamed. "Wake up! The plane is leaving in an hour!"

He opened the door a couple moments later, looking like hell. I gave him a big hug to share my enthusiasm. It was 5:40.

"Let's go, man! We cannot miss this flight!"

I grabbed everything that was in the room and stuffed it into my backpack. Whatever didn't fit in mine, I threw in Jackson's. I was yelling and moving at top speed the whole time. I was like a coked-up motivational trainer trying to win a race.

"We are going to make it! Hurry! We are not going to miss this flight!"

Jackson was still half asleep through the whole thing. I convinced him to just follow me, and we bolted out the door. Jackson and I ran down the street and jumped into the first taxi we saw.

"I will give you forty Euros and one hundred dollars to take us to the airport as fast as possible."

We left Munich the same way we had entered, going over one hundred miles an hour. The taxi pulled up at the front of the airport at 6:20, I threw the cash into the front seat, and we sprinted inside. As fast as we were going, international customs still took their time. Once through, there was another mad dash through the terminal.

Jackson and I reached the gate at 6:55. We didn't have time to think, and we each raced to the nearest trashcan and hurled our guts out. I was completely out of breath as I handed the agent my ticket. I reached my seat inside the plane, and my head was spinning. After taking in some deep breaths, I reached some kind of poise.

"Jackson, that was the best trip of my life."

Jackson was already passed out next to me. I sat back and closed my eyes. I couldn't fall asleep right now. This was too much of a high. The plane moved down the runway and took off.

Thoughts were few and far between.

I do remember thinking, "I'm on my way home; how am I ever going to top a trip like that?"

16

So what happened after such an amazing trip? It's hard to say, but I do know it expanded my personal sense of invincibility. This would later be both to my detriment and betterment. There are a couple of more stories to share, along with where I am today and where I'm going tomorrow.

The rest of the summer, I continued to work at Home Cookin'. I saved my money and drove six hours to see my college buddies at Atlantic Beach, North Carolina. Right when I got there, one of my friends, Johnny, bought a two hundred dollar vaporizer. We rode around the beach, stopping at different houses and taking donations of pot to put in the new contraption. It looked like a power tool with a tube.

There were a group of girls living at the beach that summer that we had grown close to over our freshmen year. Their house was called the Pink House, and it had been passed down over the summers as a designated party locale.

In the spring semester, I had spent a good amount of time with Betsy, a cute girl from my dorm. We spent many nights together, but I gave the relationship the axe before the summer, mainly to pursue the girls surrounding the World Cup. She said she would come visit me in Ellington, but I simply said it's not going to happen.

Verbatim: "We live five floors from each other now, and five hours just isn't going to work."

Cold, but honest.

Well, I stayed in touch with Betsy when I got back, and she happened to be going to the beach the same weekend as me. I pushed the reuniting thoughts into the back of my mind, and I mainly focused on getting back in touch with my other friends from school.

After getting some drinks in my system, I couldn't resist. It also didn't help that she was calling me every thirty minutes to come over to the Pink House. In Buddy Applegate fashion, I had a handle of Seagrams Seven and Sprite. Johnny was driving, and we pulled up to the house.

Uncharacteristically, Johnny was kind of hesitant. The vaporizer may have had something to do with that. I, on the other hand, thought I was king of the world. I chugged my beer in the front seat and reached in the back to grab more liquid courage.

Without hesitation, I carried that handle up the stairs and busted through the front door. Eight good-looking girls were standing there, and they all screamed when they saw me, each one coming up in succession to hug me. Betsy waited her turn, trying to hide her excitement.

The night went on, with me bragging about the trip I just had. My head had gotten so big, I'm surprised I didn't float away. The night grew late, and Betsy was still in the mix. Next move, outdoor shower.

We spent a lot of time in the shower between the suite of dorms, and this was a perfect reunion. The air was cool, and the warm water felt good flowing over us. After doing our thing, we grabbed some blankets and fell asleep outside in a hammock.

I stayed at the beach a couple of more days, and watched the final of the World Cup with some more friends at a family vacation house.

Italy and France played to a 1-1 draw and ended the match in penalty kicks. The famous French striker David Trezeguet skied the last shot over the bar, and the Italians were the victors. The month-long tournament was over. In another four years, South Africa would host the next one. I guess I had some kind of sinking feeling of closure, but that trip to Germany was really just the beginning of the end.

————————————

The rest of the summer flew by, and I moved into the fraternity house that August. That was interesting to say the least. It was a constant party, and I loved it. Rush, bands, socials, and football games all allowed me to get as drunk and stoned as possible. Luckily, I didn't really get into other drugs that heavily. I guess.

Through mutual friends, I came across a guy that I made instant friends with: Maxwell Francis Marshall. He was from Lookout Mountain, Tennessee, and he was at UNC on a wrestling scholarship. Rumor had it, he took the SAT five times to break 800, back when it was a 1600-point test. Max was right up there with Gator in wild lifestyle, things I was attracted to for the wrong reasons.

One afternoon, I saw Max coming back from class, and he asked if I wanted to go out to eat for his birthday. I couldn't turn it down. Five of us went to a burger and wing joint around the corner. We ran up a $320 tab between five people. It seemed like we ordered every shot they had. Sitting in the corner, we were breaking glasses and trying not to fall out of our chairs.

It was eight o'clock, and I was starting to black out. Max and I went back to my fraternity house, punched holes in the wall, and left. When I was drunk, sometimes I just felt like being as destructive as possible.

Then, we went next door to Maxwell's fraternity house. They had a ton of cardboard behind the dumpster. I lit it on fire and danced in the flames. This was not the brightest idea for a significant reason. Our fraternity house had burned down on Mother's Day about ten years earlier. It was the biggest fire in Chapel Hill history; five students had died. Just mentioning fire was disrespectful, let alone starting one so close by the house. My drunken action was a slap in the face to the long-standing traditions and painful recovery from that horrific night. I was slowly losing my mind.

Of course, their president tried to stop the commotion. Others got out the hose, I cussed the president out, and Max pulled around the corner in his truck. I hopped in the front seat and held my middle finger out to everyone I could see.

Chapel Hill is a small town, and it doesn't take long to get into the country. Max flew down those back roads, and I just sat there like it was no big deal. I gazed over at the speedometer, and it read ninety. I mean, what's the worst that can happen on a curving, two-lane highway, right? We went through a cornfield too.

I distinctly remember Yonder Mountain String Band's "Half Moon Rising" playing as loud as possible. I absolutely did not give a fuck what happened. We made it back to Chapel Hill, and I passed out cold like many times before.

My lifestyle was starting to spin out of control. One of the bowling balls I had been holding for so long was about to drop. The competition at school was fierce, and my self-confidence was dwindling. These benders were outlets for my inability to reach perfection. Underneath the surface, I was a scared boy with low self-esteem who was running from himself and that unaddressed fear of alcohol controlling his life.

I was drinking more often and drinking more each time I drank. Anything was good enough of an excuse to booze it up. You have to understand, my behavior may seem to be a little wild, but in the world of fraternity life, almost everything is overlooked. The same was true of Ellington. There are some that may be reading this thinking all of this was amateurish. I wasn't the top of the totem pole in getting fucked up, but I was starting to develop a problem—actually, multiple problems.

First, the damn whiskey dick kept catching up with me. Being exposed to so many girls gave me ample opportunities to hop in the sack. I wasn't killing it, but girls were steady. Everything was fine until whiskey dick would come knocking on my door at the wrong time. On multiple occasions, I would have a girl ready to go, but it would not work out. The conversation usually went something like this:

"What's the matter, Cam?"

I would slur drunkenly, "Baby, just give me a minute."

"I'm naked and on top of you. Am I not turning you on? I don't understand."

Internal dialogue: No, bitch, you wouldn't understand. I have been drinking all day, which helped me get you in this position but it is now preventing me from completing the mission.

Actual response: "Sweetheart, the whiskey dick got me again."

"The whiskey what?"

"This ain't going to work tonight. Pretend like something cool happened in the morning."

"Um . . . okay."

That, my friends, was my anticlimactic and sexually deteriorating experience of whiskey dick. Every guy that's gone a little wild should know what I'm talking about. The key to life is balance, and whiskey dick doesn't fit into that equation. As I was saying, this was only one of my developing troubles.

The football games were starting to wear me out. Drinking bourbon and gingers and screwdrivers all day led to steady blackouts. When people were throwing the football out in the yard on a sunny afternoon, I would be in my dark room, looking out the window. Everything started to take on a darker tone. My body movements slowed down, and my day-to-day thought process wasn't as sharp.

At least I went out with a bang. Gator had a good friend from home at Appalachian State University. Trey Anastasio was playing crunchy guitar, and Gator raced up there on an early Thursday in November to see him. As the lead guitarist in the renowned band Phish, how could Gator miss it? The next day, Johnny, Andy, and I were on the way to Boone for a fun-filled weekend.

We all left Chapel Hill late Friday afternoon and went west into the mountains. As we pulled out of the fraternity house parking lot, my iPod was blaring Velvet Underground's "Rock and Roll." By the time we got to Boone, it was cold as hell.

I'm not going to lie, I remember very little of that weekend. We went to a football game, we spent all day in a bar, I hooked up with a girl, and I told her I never wanted to see her again. I had reached the epitome of a drunken asshole, but I wouldn't admit that to the mirror if I tried. We got back from Boone on Sunday, and I left Chapel Hill on Tuesday.

I had become so disoriented from so many drugs and drinking and so little sleep, I was delirious. Nobody knew what to do. I needed help, and I ended up flying home because I was in no shape to drive. Thinking that I just needed a break, my bag for the flight was light. It didn't even have any pants in it. I didn't come back to North Carolina for six months.

Gator and I had become pretty close by then. I think my departure shook him up a little bit. I don't think it was all related to me, but he decided to take a break from Chapel Hill as well, and he returned to his eastern North Carolina home for a couple of months. He was back the next semester.

On November 11, 2006, I began the long process of getting sober. I had an iron will including a lot of naivety, and I wanted to go back to Chapel Hill immediately. Despite my impatience, I wouldn't be ready for quite some time. It took me over a year to get back to UNC.

I never went to any kind of rehab program. It was cold turkey. While drying out for the first time in my life, every shell and layer of self-confidence melted away. I had reached a pinnacle of a charismatic lifestyle, only to find it was full of holes and pitfalls. I had lost everything that I thought was important, and my world had been turned upside down.

I was scared to death of what people would think of me up at school. I had literally disappeared. I turned my phone off in November and didn't turn it back on until around Christmas. Friends had called in concern but couldn't get through. They left voice mails in troubled but uncertain voices.

After mustering up some form of courage, I listened to the many voice mails people had left during my absence. Other people I knew from school weren't sure how to react, and I never heard from them.

Betsy's was one of the first messages I heard. After the horrible way I treated her, she still cared about me. I used her, and I was ashamed of that. For her to call me only looking to help made me feel even worse. I was beginning to look in the mirror for the first time in my life, and I really didn't like what was looking back at me. I called many of my friends back and lied out of fear that I would be back the next semester.

Jackson heard about everything and came to see me over Christmas. I hadn't showered for a couple of days. I was wearing pajama pants, bedroom slippers, and a ratty white undershirt. It was pitiful. He was at a loss for words.

I think it was painful for him to look at me. This was his friend, the one he had conquered Europe with, the one who pushed forward everything forbidden and made it okay, the one he laughed with. Damn, the one he shared a single bed in a whorehouse with. My eyes were sunken in my skull, my hair was greasy, and I couldn't crack a smile to save my life. He left with hollow words of encouragement. I don't know how much hope he had for me to get back to my old self.

On top of all of this, I had a closet packed full of skeletons. I won't get into all of the details, but there were deep issues regarding childhood traumas with male figures. I guess Dr. Traugott was right. I was in deep agony, and I cried intensely for weeks, maybe months. It was the first time I had shown that kind of emotion and vulnerability in my life. As painful as this breakdown was at the time, it was a much-needed and long-overdue form of catharsis.

Every Tuesday, Thursday, and Saturday, I would have anxiety attacks. These were the days that I went out up at school. Now that I was dead sober, I didn't have any way to escape. I felt like I was going to jump out of my skin. It was awful.

Nevertheless, I believed I had an iron will. I was not going to let this terrible darkness defeat me. I was already working against the odds of family genetics and poor personal choices, but I was determined to dig myself out of this hole. Now, I was beginning to understand why my mom had warned me so many times before.

My mother was the main benefactor of my rehabilitation back to health. Unbeknownst to me, Mom had seen the direct effect of alcohol during her marriage. My father had his own personal demons that he could not escape, including the bottle. With great integrity, Mom explained the situation in a loving way. Dad had actually been sober for two years before the car accident. Before that, he struggled many times to finally stop drinking. Dad finally accomplished his goal of sobriety, but his life was cut short by the actions of another who had the same problem that he had overcome.

Mom's devotion to my father throughout the hard times was baffling to me. However, I now understand that when she took her vows for marriage, she believed in "until death do us part." I now have no doubt that my father was a good man. I could see that Mom's judgments were candid, and her perseverance was inexorable. This was because of her faith.

Being around my mother while I was recovering helped me understand her tremendous compassion and resilience in the midst of suffering. The amount of love she provided is indescribable. Her determination and will power for my recovery gave me strength that I did not have.

Mom didn't put any pressure on me other than to get well. I gardened, I read, I watched movies. Mainly, I slept. I was depressed in every sense of the word, but I was getting better as time passed. Springtime lifted my spirits some.

Mom was a saint through the whole thing. She constantly encouraged me that "time is the great healer". Regardless of her reassuring words, I know it was extremely tough to watch her only child suffer in such a way. There were points where she was simply helpless. Under her guidance, we did get into a routine of reading devotionals in the morning.

I had attended church since I was a little kid. However, this dynamic of faith and despair took on a completely different meaning. Up until this point, tests were a breeze, socializing was natural, and sports came easy.

I can only describe my struggle like a burning candle. Imagine a flickering candle in a dark cave. The wind comes through, and the flame is about to go out. That was the only amount of hope I had to make it through. But it was enough, and I am ever grateful for that. Even if the devotional readings didn't seem to help at the time, I know they were affecting my attitude toward recovery.

Throughout the early part of the year, I would call my friends at school and tell them I was coming to visit for the weekend. Every time Friday would roll around, I got too nervous to make the five-hour drive. I chickened out and stayed in the safety net of Ellington. Finally, I made my way back in May, and John was with me the whole way.

The first time John heard about me leaving school, he said he was going to drop out to come home and take care of me. He wasn't really going to do this, but I wouldn't have been surprised if he did. He was just that kind of friend. Since Columbia was en route to Chapel Hill, he agreed to travel with me right before the spring semester ended. We planned on going up after the last day of classes and before exams.

I was nervous the whole way. I thought I would be shamed by everybody I knew. Pulling up to the fraternity house felt like diving back into the lion's den. When we got there, Bueller was laying on a couch in the front yard. Beer cans were spread over the yard like they had rained down from the sky.

I had finally made it back, and I don't think anybody really thought I was going to return. After seeing a couple of old buddies, it was like I never left. Another factor that helped was the timing. Since we arrived after the last class, everybody was hungover from the night before. This was good because there was no alcohol around.

Of course, I let Betsy know I was coming back. She was glad to see me, and John and I stayed with her. I really don't know how she put up with me, but I'm glad for her support and kindness. I left the next day even more encouraged and inspired to make it back to UNC.

During my time at home, my family was extremely supportive, especially my grandparents and my uncle. My uncle was the lawyer at a large law office. He gave me a job running errands. It wasn't a glorious job, but it gave me a sense of accomplishment. I still wanted to return to

Chapel Hill as soon as possible, but I had to prove I could handle school again first.

I went to the college in Ellington for the 2007 fall semester. I really started to take my health seriously, and I was working out four times a week. Other than playing sports in high school every day, this was the most physically healthy I had been in my life.

That Christmas, I counted down the days until I would actually move back to North Carolina. I found a roommate through the grapevine, and we lived in an apartment close to campus. I was as motivated as ever.

I was still fixated on Betsy, but another girl came into the picture. Her name was Josephine, but everyone called her Josey. I met her on an online dating website called RelationswithRecovery.com. It was great for me at the time. The website was set up for recovering alcoholics to meet girls who sympathized with dysfunction. You just sign up and listed the day you got sober in your profile. When potential partners look over your profile, an electronic clock increases your sobriety by the second. I was low in recovery time, but I had a killer profile picture, so Josey took the bait (completely kidding; if we met like that, I couldn't look myself in the mirror).

I first met her at the beach the summer before my freshman year. We both snuck into a bar, and shagged for a couple of songs. She was wearing a very flattering red floral dress. She said that she was intimidated by me, most of it coming from the alcohol I had consumed. I wasn't particularly close with Josey during my freshman or sophomore year, but we both knew each other. Later on, I distinctly remember her showing genuine concern toward me on one of my visits back to Chapel Hill before I finally returned to school.

It was funny how we started dating each other. She came to a party at the fraternity house, and she asked for a drink. The keg had floated, and I was holding a Coke. It looked like a mixed drink, and she kept asking for a sip. I wouldn't let her have any, mainly because it was just a Coke and I was too self-conscious to let her know that I had stopped drinking. But people chase what they can't have. It was a simple incident, but we were attracted to each other from that point on.

Josey was a firecracker. She was sweet as can be, half Cuban and half Mexican. She had the Latino heat. There was never a dull moment. She was a beautiful girl with a great personality and a body to die for. She had family from Spain, and one of her sisters had blonde hair and blue eyes. She really grew on me.

As time went by, Josey and I spent more and more time together, and Betsy faded out of the picture. I think Betsy was finally over my inconsistencies, and I don't blame her. I wouldn't have put up with me either. There are so many people in college. You don't want to miss out on the company of other suitable people.

Regardless, I was completely open with Josey about what I went through. She didn't judge, and she showed more and more care the closer we got. She had been through some tough times herself, and she could relate. Her oldest sister had died in a car wreck the previous year, a tragedy that many college students never come close to experiencing. It was also something we could relate to on a deeper level.

I couldn't help but have a little resentment over the fact that most other people seemed to have few qualms in their lives. Deep down, I knew other people were struggling in some way, but I always considered mine to be of bigger magnitude. I guess the grass is always greener on the other side.

Josey and I took frequent trips out of town. Very early on, we rented a cabin in the mountains and spent a wonderful and relaxing weekend in the wine country. Yes, perfect place to go for a recovering alcoholic, right? We hiked and stayed active. I was looking to have some fun, and the temptation was too much. Maybe if the cabin didn't have a hot tub, I could have resisted. I ended up sharing a couple bottles of wine. Josey didn't know that I had completely stopped drinking, so it was not a shock to her. In retrospect, I had fallen off the wagon, but I didn't have any immediate repercussions, so I didn't think too much of it.

Josey also had a beach house on Bald Head Island, and we went there regularly. In order to get on the island, you had to take a ferry. The island was very preserved, and the only way to travel anywhere was on a golf cart. It was such a relief not to be stuck in Chapel Hill every weekend.

My relationship with Josey truly helped me get readjusted to life away from Ellington. I opened up to her, and she opened up to me. That summer, I stayed in Chapel Hill and took a class in Italian film. Josey and I had almost no responsibilities, and I was living off the family dime.

We spent every day together. It was one of the best summers of my life. Nevertheless, there were some downsides to the relationship, like anyone, I guess.

Josey liked to be social, something I tried to curb in an attempt to control my drinking. After nine months, I was becoming more self-centered. I tried to change some of her behavior to suit my own problems. This was unfair to her, but I felt like if I wanted to change and uphold a new lifestyle, we needed to separate. After nine months of dating, I broke up with her.

It was one of the hardest things I've ever had to do. I still cared about her deeply, but I just needed a break. Relationships can be a tricky thing. After getting so close to somebody, letting go can be a hard. Josey was able to move on quicker than me, and I tried to remain friends over the years. Dating and friendship with girls is a fine line to walk. I knew this deep down, and I believe it ended for a reason. After the breakup, our conversations and interactions were sporadic, but getting sober had to be a personal battle. I had to stand on my own before finding the next significant other.

Even so, the strategy for complete lifestyle change actually backfired a bit. The familiar saying "Old habits die hard" came back into play. I was back in full force with partying.

Over Christmas break, I reunited with Jackson and went balls to the wall in Atlanta. I just couldn't resist, and this was disconcerting. I just pushed it away again.

Jackson and I went to a pizza place to grab dinner. I ordered pitcher after pitcher of beer, and we decided to scalp tickets for a Sound Tribe concert. I wasn't really into their music, but it sounded like fun.

Jackson asked me to take it easy that night. No matter how hard he tried, I would not listen.

We left the pizza place and pulled up to a parking lot near the venue. It was the night before New Year's Eve, and people had come from all over to see the band. There were a lot of those whacked-out people who had annoyed me at Bonaroo.

After we scalped some tickets, we made our way to the back of the line. I was wasted, but as you know, I have a tendency to mess with people.

As we walked past the young crowd eager to get inside, I just started yelling obscenities; then I yelled out, "Man, I love drugs! I took so much acid today! I am tripping my balls off right now!"

I isolated one guy with long hair and told him I had traveled all the way from Alaska to see the band. I could give two flips about the band honestly, but some people cheered at my comments.

While standing in line, there were a couple of girls in front of me, not too attractive to my recollection.

I blurted out, "Hey! Girls! You ever smoke meth?"

"No, you creep. Leave us alone."

"You should really try it. I'm on it right now, and it's making you two actually look attractive. Boogie woogie."

"You are such an asshole. Get away from us."

Jackson apologized on my behalf, and he managed to keep me somewhat tame until the concert started. Once again, another blur of a night. Despite my obvious problems, I had one thing slowly working in my favor. Thank God for my friend David.

David Ibravic was another person from Ellington who was attending UNC. His family was from the former Czechoslovakia. I did not know him in high school, but I met him my junior year during Thanksgiving. He had gone to a conservative, private high school, and he had a tremendous Christian faith. He invited me to a Bible study, and I starting going weekly beginning in January of 2009, right after my Atlanta adventure.

Now there is something everyone must understand. The three most addictive things in the world are drugs, alcohol, and religion. I was careful not to swing too far in the other direction on the pendulum of drug addict and Bible beater. I was really trying to keep a balanced life, so I attended these studies with caution. Slowly, I was becoming convicted of my behavior and developing a closer relationship with God. This didn't mean I had slowed down yet either. I was really living a double life.

I was still adhering to my Catholic upbringing, and I remember one day in particular. It was the day before Ash Wednesday, the beginning of Lent. During Lent, people give up things until Easter. My goal was to give up drugs and alcohol. But I justified one last hurrah before the forty days of abstinence.

We had a Bible study on a Tuesday night, and I went straight to a bar after we finished. I pounded liquor drinks like there was no tomorrow. I was in the grips of addictive behavior, and I chased that high all night. I stayed up until five in the morning, blowing coke for the first time in my life.

This may not seem like a huge ordeal to many, but given my past experience, it was quite frightening. Once again, I ignored the obvious and just went and played nine holes of golf the next day. Secretly, I wished Josey was still around, but I knew I had to tackle my personal demons on my own.

There was a streak at school that really took a toll. North Carolina was a favorite to win the national championship in basketball that year. UNC has one of the most historical programs in the sport, and the fans are very devoted. Growing up watching SEC football, I didn't really understand the obsession with basketball. I learned quickly, and I hopped on the bandwagon. At UNC, basketball was king.

The stretch of tournament games during March Madness was party central. There was so much excitement about the chances of the team. The whole school rallied. We made it to the national championship game and won by seventeen. Thousands rushed to the middle of town at Franklin Street. John had driven up with some friends, and we joined the madness, dancing around bonfires and weaving in and out of the enormous and rowdy crowd.

Everybody was letting loose that night. Maxwell was in a bar that overlooked the main town corner and tried to dump a glass of urine on the people below. They actually had to carry him out because when they caught him, he played dead. He ended up scaling a column from the street and walking on top of a building clapping his hands. There was film of him shot by a news helicopter.

Needless to say, there was no shortage of partying that semester. I continued the streak up until our formal in late spring. We had all been working tirelessly building the exotic hut for our formal.

The Sunday after the biggest weekend of debauchery of the year, something hit me. I woke up that morning and decided I had enough. Not in a fanatical way, but I knew God was telling me something. I truly believe everything I went through was to humble me and prevent me from going down a destructive path for the rest of my life. I made a full commitment on April 19, 2009, to stay sober for the rest of my life. Keep reading and take it to heart.

17

I still had another year left in school, and it was extremely trying. Most of my friends had graduated, and I isolated myself in many ways to prevent any temptations of relapse. I tried Alcoholics Anonymous, but it just wasn't for me. I actually went to my first meeting after being sober for six months. That's the tricky part about living without alcohol. It's not getting sober, it's staying sober. I was just looking for support.

I understood the concept of AA, but I really wanted to have privacy in how I dealt with lifestyle choices. It was depressing to hear other people's horror stories with alcohol, and I didn't want to be scared into sobriety. For those people who do utilize AA, I think that is great. Whatever they need to do to keep them sober and create a better life is fine. It just wasn't what I felt comfortable with.

That fall, I ended up leading a Bible study at the fraternity house. This was unthinkable when I was younger, but having seniority gave me more freedom in decisions. Others looked at it strangely, but it was a good outlet for the younger kids. I didn't want them to make the same mistakes I had made, and it really helped me as well.

I took some entrepreneurship classes, and I had some different opportunities present themselves. A doctor's office from Ellington was heavily involved with technology, and they were trying to get a small biotech company off the ground. Chapel Hill is a great place for scientific and medical businesses, and the group of doctors asked me to help make some contacts. I also got hooked up with another science company involved with toxicology. Contributing to those ventures helped me deter old behavior.

Believe it or not, I also got to know a girl that fall while being completely sober. I picked her up at a bar too.

My first sober girl was named Sarah, but I called her Cocoa because she sold Hershey's chocolate. Plus she had a nice ass, not unlike some dark-skinned females. Cocoa already graduated from a college in Texas, she had a job, and she was a year older than me. Man, was I cougar hunting or what?

As I progressed in my sobriety, I replaced my cravings for alcohol with nicotine. It calmed my nerves, so I just sucked down a cigarette whenever I started getting anxious. I developed a nasty smoking habit and went through at least a pack a day. Because of my excessive tobacco use, I started to wheeze a good bit.

While I was with Cocoa, I found out that wheezing heavily is not a turn-on in the bedroom. To remedy the burden, I actually bought an inhaler and made a necklace so I could wear it when things got too hectic. When I was butt naked giving it hell, I had three things dangling, my two balls and my inhaler (just kidding). But I did have to catch my breath more than usual during our rendezvous.

The short time with Cocoa was good while it lasted. She actually broke up with me, which was a first in my life. I was looking for emotional support way too early in the relationship, if I could call it that. I believe being vulnerable so quickly with Cocoa was intimidating and scared her off. A sober twenty-two-year-old is rare, and it's intriguing at first but also raises some red flags.

She was not able to open up to me like I wanted, and I know it was because I rushed it. It would have been nice to hang out with her, but she ignored me completely. Weakness and neediness may not have been good enough for her at the time.

Being dumped not long after getting sober was not the best experience in the world. Trust me. Experts recommend not getting into any kind of relationship, whatever form that might be, for at least a year.

My self-confidence was down to my toes to begin with, and a good kick in the balls from a cute girl made it even worse. But you know, I stuck myself out there, and that's what happens sometimes. Maybe Cocoa cut it off with me because of the wheezing too.

I knew then how it felt to be rejected. After that experience, I was able to sympathize with the girls from the past. Yeah, great tradeoff and life lesson. Thank you, karma.

———————————

I finished up my last semester the spring of 2010 at UNC, and I only had one more class to graduate. I signed up for an online class for the fall of 2010. During that time, I moved back to Ellington, ran a soccer academy for an elementary school, worked on a political campaign, and substitute taught at a high school.

I stayed busy, but it was not a demanding schedule. It allowed me to focus on that very last class and come to terms with all of the events that had transpired over the last four years. I still had my old friends, and I made some new ones as well.

Other extracurricular activities included attending a Bible study once a week and playing soccer in an adult league. I went out to bars but just drank ginger ale. I have to admit, I hopped on the Red Bull train somewhat. If you drink too many of those at once, it's like being on speed. I tried to limit those kinds of nights, but every now and then, I would let loose. Other than smoking a half a pack of cigarettes a day, that is the craziest I have gotten. Funny transformation from a three-week bender at the beginning of the story.

Why was I so afraid to look in the mirror? Deep down, I was ashamed of who I had become. I was blessed with great opportunities and gifts. Instead of utilizing them for something good, I was selfish. I took the money I had earned over the years and squandered it on the things of the world like drugs and alcohol. They gave me temporary satisfaction, but it wasn't the fulfillment I was looking for. My constant search for something more was the result of never feeling completely accepted. And I've learned that it is impossible to find perfect acceptance without looking to something greater than myself.

That begs the question, who will accept me? Once I realized my shortcomings and realized that whatever I did was never going to be flawless, I was able to find comfort in that fact that God has everlasting acceptance. He loves people despite their inconsistencies and failures.

It took me a long time to realize this simple fact. You may be thinking "Whoa there, Joel Osteen," but damn it, this stuff is important, so listen.

Some people don't have a concept of who God is and how everything works. There are roadblocks to developing a faith. There are doctrines in churches along with behavior of so-called Christians that make the whole concept controversial and meaningless. It's completely understandable to have doubt about all of the things that I am proposing. But keep it simple. We aren't perfect, God is, and He always forgives us.

When I came home, the first person who came to see me was my godfather, my dad's younger brother Timothy. As he sat down to talk to me for the first time since I left Chapel Hill, he could tell I was strung out and worried. I was completely convinced that I had shamed the Montclair family. Unexpectedly, our conversation blew my mind and brought me to the verge of tears. First, he told me this story:

"There was a boy who asked for his father's inheritance to travel to a foreign land. The boy wanted to enjoy the luxuries of life, and he squandered his inheritance on wild times. When the money was gone, he went to the farmers to try and find shelter and food. He was so poor that he worked with the pigs and ate with them. The son came to the realization that his father's workers lived a better life than him, so he returned home to ask for a job from his father. At the end of his journey home, the father saw him from a distance and ran toward him. The son was worn from his hard times, but the father put him in his arms and comforted him. The father said, 'Quick! Bring the best robe and put it on him. Put a ring on his finger and sandals on his feet. Bring the fattened calf and kill it. Let's have a feast and celebrate. For this son of mine was dead and is alive again; he was lost and is found.'"

"But Uncle Tim, why would the father accept him again?"

"Cam, this is the parable of the Prodigal Son. The story is about how God treats us. No matter how far we fall away from him, he is always there to welcome us back with open arms."

I will always be able to relate to that story. In times of trial and trouble, I realize that there is comfort in a power greater than us. Through that comfort, we are able to help other people who may have had a similar trying experience. The very thing that seems to constrain us is actually the source of our own liberation. This is how I found my freedom.

So what is in store for this changed twenty-three-year-old? Believe it or not, Brazil is next on the list. Yes, the 2014 World Cup. This opportunity is due to Harry, my old high school friend. I told you he would come back into the picture. Harry is a year older than me and graduated from the University of Georgia. After college, he landed a sweet investment banking job.

His job didn't start until June of 2009, and he had six months to himself. Harry went to Argentina by himself for four of those months. He didn't know Spanish or anything about South America, but he took a chance and had the time of his life. He shared some stories with me, some of them matching my time in Germany but in other ways.

One time, he decided to go camping for ten days. Harry wanted to have time to himself, but he almost died in the process. Without a compass or general idea of where he was, he made it seven days in the wilderness but got lost in the process. He took the wrong trail and basically met a life-or-death situation. He had vague memories of the trail he came in on, but he was lost. Harry picked a direction and pushed through miles of thick brush and bamboo toward some form of civilization. He suffered cuts and bruises, leaving him hungry, bloody, and battered.

Miraculously, he finally made it out and found a small hostel. He walked in the door, looking like he had come out of a war. The Argentinean women running the hostel quickly came to his aid and cared for him.

The owners of the hostel fed him and washed his clothes. Since those were the only clothes he had, they let him borrow one of the women's nightgowns. He sat downstairs in a nightgown and ate a much-needed home-cooked meal. Who could forget a story like that?

During his travels, he met up with a Scottish guy and an Australian guy. They all decided to travel together, and each one acted as a translator in order to communicate between the trio. They were all speaking English, but the dialect was so strong for each, only one could understand the other at a time. I think that's pretty funny.

Harry has been working eighty hours a week for the past two years. He is leaving his high-paying job in New York City and moving to Brazil to open up a hostel.

He and a college friend are leaving in August to live in Rio de Janeiro for nine months, doing whatever jobs they can find. Once acclimated to the country and its culture, his high powered team will be investing in a venture to prepare for the influx of people during the World Cup. I will be visiting them for another adventure in the summer of 2014.

Harry walks to the beat of his own drum. This is something I look for in any close friend. Jackson, Gator, Bueller, and John all do it too.

In the meantime, I have grown in my aspirations for my future career. It may seem hard to believe given my recklessness and stupidity at the beginning of the book, but I have had a lot of time for true self-reflection and personal growth. I view the world through a different lens now.

My perspective has broadened to a point where I can see others' problems with abuse and self-destruction developing long before they come to full fruition. I was lucky enough to survive my adolescent lifestyle, and I have empathy for those who struggle to climb out of the darkness and despair of the life I used to live.

There is a reason I survived and came out on the other side. My revelation of personal security is evident in the first verses of 2 Corinthians, "³Praise be to the God and Father of our Lord Jesus Christ, the Father of compassion and the God of all comfort, ⁴ who comforts us in all our troubles, so that we can comfort those in any trouble with the comfort we ourselves receive from God." Once again, this may seem like I have swung to the other side of the pendulum between addict and Bible beater, but this is a practical way to live that is very rewarding. You don't have to be a diehard Christian to apply these principles. Basically, take what you have learned and share it with others who need that knowledge and wisdom.

My Mom displayed this form of altruism when she was taking care of me. Our family dynamics were not the most favorable, but she persevered and kept a positive outlook on life. She was able to comfort me in my suffering because she had received comfort after my father's death.

When I was searching for something more in my life, I was aimless. I grasped at straws of impulsivity and instant gratification to fill a void. It always felt like something was missing. I needed guidance, a leader who I could respect in that part of my life. There was so much appeal in the unhealthy and destructive highs; it put me in a place of helplessness.

Does everybody that's ever experienced a high need help? No, but it is a problem that is growing and more evident as time passes. It is important to note that personal change cannot be forced. An individual that has a problem is the only person who can fix the problem.

I know my calling is to guide others in a positive direction before they get into a place they cannot escape. I was lucky. Hell, I'm fortunate to be alive.

This may come as a surprise as well. Before the next World Cup, I will have completed a Masters in Clinical Psychology. This doesn't mean I can save the world by any means. But the human psyche is fascinating. It twists and turns everyday as we face the entire spectrum of emotions. These emotions facilitate actions that, over time, develop behaviors. As much as I don't want to admit it, Dr. Traugott read me like a book in fifteen minutes.

I don't believe everybody needs to lie on a couch to come to terms with struggles in their life. Still, the most important thing is to be able to look in the mirror and be completely honest with what you see. My educational pursuits are a personal endeavor so I can better understand the way the mind works. It is the starting line of a marathon. Through meditation and study, I have realized that the wisest man is not the one that knows everything; it is the man that realizes he knows nothing.

Hopefully, this book will show the temptations in the world, the insights that are possible, and a life of peace. The search for self is a lifelong process, but I know I'm on the right path.

———————————

Would I trade any part of this book to not go through the hard times? It's tempting to say yes, but in the end, I would only take back the times I hurt other people through my inconsiderate behavior. I saw an interesting documentary about a man who had been a prisoner of war during the Korean War; he spent two years in solitary isolation. It only made him stronger. He used his mind to take every brick of his house apart and reconstruct it in different ways. Once he had added on a wing, he would take that apart and start over. They asked him if he would take the experience back if he could. He full-heartedly said he would not trade it for the world.

The concept of suffering is a hard one to grasp. Why does it happen? If there is a God, why does he allow suffering? We have an esteemed professor at UNC, Isaac Moore, who teaches religious studies. He went to seminary at Oxford, and now he is an atheist. He challenges his students to question their faith. I went to a debate, and honestly, he was pretty convincing that a loving God should not allow any suffering.

But I've been through it, the highs and the lows. Not to be a downer, but at some point in your life, there will be tough times. How will you react when everything seems to be going against you? Will you feel guilty for the things you have done?

Suffering allows you to look forward to the times when things will be good again, right? I tend to disagree. If you can still find joy in the midst of suffering, you have mastered the art. No matter what comes your way, you can be adept to handle it. Plain and simple, your character will shine through the darkest hours.

I have written a book about the wild times I have had, but this story is about more than just getting wasted. Sow your wild oats. But then, it's time to move on.

Down deep, what do you rely on? Are you a good person? Would you be there for your friends and family? There are so many examples that I shared of unconditional love through friendship and support from family. I'm not anywhere close to perfect, but I take solace in the fact that I'm trying to be a better person.

If you didn't put the book down after I got on the plane back to Ellington, I applaud you. The World Cup was one of the most amazing experiences of my life. As always, I encourage people to explore new territories. But don't go so far in search of freedom that you lose yourself in the process. Some people never come back from the search for self, and they are absolutely hollow inside. They have tombstones in their eyes. The thing they are looking for is in their gut the whole time, but they miss it somehow. This may seem grim, but it's the truth.

The main thing that comes to mind about what I have learned is a line by Bob Dylan: "You don't need a weatherman to know which way the wind blows." Human instinct is a powerful tool, and the gut knows much more than we give it credit. Rely on it and see what happens.

Good luck,
Cam